CRAZ

"Ever see a genuine, in the flesh, _____ before?" Karen demanded.

"I'm not sure." Piper shrugged. "I don't think so."

"Then feast your eyes on this!" Karen smugly handed over the binoculars and crawled to the corner of the hedge.

Piper nearly gasped out loud. There, walking down the road, was the most gorgeous boy she had ever seen. Tall and muscular, he was wearing crisp white shorts, a matching cotton boatneck sweater, spotless tennis shoes that showed off his perfect tan, and he carried a tennis racket under his arm. With his sun-streaked hair and sunglasses dangling from his neck, he looked like an advertisement for *Esquire*.

"He's perfect!" Piper fell back on the grass.

"And he's coming this way!" Karen hissed from the side of the hedge. "Don't move!"

Bantam Sweet Dreams Romances
Ask your bookseller for the books you have missed

Crazy For You

Jahnna Beecham

BANTAM BOOKS
TORONTO · NEW YORK · LONDON · SYDNEY · AUCKLAND

RL 6, IL age 11 and up

CRAZY FOR YOU
A Bantam Book/April 1989

ISBN 0-553-27125-3

Published simultaneously in the United States and Canada

Printed and bound in Great Britain by
Cox & Wyman Ltd., Reading

*For our Maine-iac friends: John, Lizzy,
Eric, Jane, Bob, and the Wrays*

Chapter One

Piper Elliot pulled her bike to the side of the road and cupped her hands around her mouth. "Karen! Stop!"

Karen wobbled precariously on her bike as she looked behind her, then swung around in a wide arc and pedaled back up the road toward Piper.

"Over here!" Piper urged, gesturing to the overlook above the bay. "Just for a minute!"

"Piper! We're going to be late for work!" Karen complained, pointing to the watch wrapped around her tanned arm.

Piper pushed her sleek, brown hair away from her forehead and smiled at her best friend. "Come on! We've got time. It's a perfect summer day. Please?"

"Oh, all right," Karen grumbled. "But just for a minute." She followed Piper off the road to the overlook where Piper was staring dreamily down at the waves beating up against the shore.

"I love it up here!" Piper said, her brown eyes sparkling in the sunlight. "I always feel like a heroine in a Gothic romance. You know, standing on the cliff, looking out to sea . . ."

"Right," Karen echoed, as though she had heard this speech before. "Wearing a beautiful white lace dress, with long, flowing hair . . ."

"Searching the horizon for a tall ship, and her handsome sea captain, who promised to return one day . . ." Piper sighed. "Now, that's romantic!"

"Yeah, and unrealistic," Karen cracked, breaking the mood. "In my entire sixteen years, I have yet to meet one handsome sea captain."

Piper chuckled. "That's the truth. There's nothing in Kittery Cove but lobsters."

"You forgot the tourists," Karen reminded her.

During the winter, Kittery Cove, Maine, was a tiny village of a few hundred local residents, but by the Fourth of July the population always swelled to several thousand as the tourists flocked to their summer homes.

Piper and Karen lived on the south side of the village where most of the permanent residents made their homes. Tidy clapboard cottages nestled around the fishing harbor, and a few lobster boats still bobbed at their moorings.

Now the girls were standing above North Harbor where the people from "away" kept their summer homes. From the overlook, Karen and Piper could peer right onto the grounds of the beautiful mansions, with their elegantly sculptured lawns and gardens.

"Look! Someone's moving into Sea Cliff!" Karen pointed toward the huge gray and white mansion that reigned splendidly over all the others.

Sea Cliff was the biggest mansion on the island and rumored to be owned by one of the wealthiest families in America. Two trucks were parked in front of the gracious Victorian structure, and workmen were scurrying back and forth, moving furniture onto the wraparound porch.

"No one has lived there for years." Piper's pulse quickened. "Let's go see who it is!" She spun her bike around and skittered off over the gravel back to the road.

"But what about work?" Karen shouted, racing to catch up with her. "We can't be late."

"It's on our way," Piper called over her shoulder. "We'll just stop for a quick peek." Piper was already pedaling down the winding road toward Sea Cliff. The wind rushed through her thick, dark hair, and with a whoop, she let go of her handlebars. Raising her arms straight up above her head, Piper coasted all the way to the bottom of the hill.

They dropped their bikes on a lawn a few

houses away from Sea Cliff and scurried across the street, slipping behind the thick hedge.

Piper pulled an old, torn leather case out of her backpack. "I knew these would come in handy someday. I've been carrying them around ever since I had to do that report on birds of coastal Maine."

"What is that?" Karen recoiled from the shredded leather box.

"Binoculars, silly. They're from Dad's boat." As she spoke, one of the leather straps came apart in her hands. "I guess the sea air kind of rotted them."

"Looks like a couple of lobsters got their claws into them, too."

"Maybe. But the insides seem to be okay." Piper quickly trained them on the mansion and fiddled with the focusing knob.

"Oh, Karen!" she gasped. "It's just as beautiful as we thought it'd be."

For years the two of them had tried to peer through the tall French windows into the house, but the shades were always tightly drawn. "There's a big, stone fireplace in the living room and a grand staircase right out of *Gone with the Wind*." Suddenly Piper let out a shrill squeal.

"What is it?" Karen pounded her on the shoulder in frustration.

"I don't believe it! They have crystal chandeliers everywhere!" Piper turned her binoculars toward the truck. "Now they're unloading wicker furniture, and a bicycle, and—"

"Let me see!" Karen yanked the binoculars out of Piper's hands and took a look. "A large bike, a basketball, weights, hmmm . . ." Finally she lowered the binoculars and announced, "A tall, muscular boy lives at Sea Cliff."

Piper's eyes widened and she whispered, "This morning, when I woke up, I had the funniest feeling that something great would happen today!"

"To you, or me?" Karen asked, polishing the lens with her shirt. "I could use something great in my life."

"I hope it's me," Piper whispered, closing her eyes tightly. "And I hope he's handsome and lives at Sea Cliff."

"He may not like locals," Karen said with a laugh. "You know how those people from away can be."

Piper's expression fell so drastically that Karen quickly added, "Relax. You're not a genuine local, anyway."

Piper drew herself up indignantly. "My family moved here when I was two years old, and we've lived here for fourteen years. How local can you get?"

Karen shook her head. "Sorry. You're still from away. If you weren't born here, you're not a true Mainer."

5

"Maniac is more like it!" Piper muttered, sticking her tongue out at Karen.

They had been having this argument for as long as Piper could remember. Karen had been born in Maine, and so had her parents, and her parents' parents. So she was definitely a "local."

"Anyway," Piper mused, "we're not even positive that a boy lives there. Those few odds and ends aren't real evidence. What do you think?"

Karen was not listening. In fact, she had the binoculars trained in the opposite direction. Suddenly she whistled between her teeth.

"Ever see a genuine, in the flesh, mega-hunk before?" Karen demanded.

"I'm not sure." Piper shrugged. "I don't think so."

"Then feast your eyes on this!" Karen smugly handed over the binoculars and crawled to the corner of the hedge.

Piper nearly gasped out loud. There, walking down the road, was the most gorgeous boy she had ever seen. Tall and muscular, he was wearing crisp white shorts, a matching cotton boat-neck sweater, spotless tennis shoes that showed off his perfect tan, and he carried a tennis racket under his arm. With his sun-streaked hair and sunglasses dangling from his neck, he looked like an advertisement for *Esquire*.

"He's perfect!" Piper fell back on the grass.

"And he's coming this way!" Karen hissed from the side of the hedge. "Don't move."

Piper, still on her back, held her breath and listened to the boy's footsteps come up the street. As he neared the hedge, Piper heard Karen say, in an unusually hoarse voice, "Hello!" An answering baritone murmured in reply.

Moments later Karen collapsed on the grass next to Piper. "He said 'hello,' " she said triumphantly, "and then he smiled at me!"

"Oh, wipe that grin off your face." Piper couldn't help feeling a little jealous of her friend's boldness.

"And his teeth match his shirt and shorts," Karen added. "Perfectly."

"I'll bet he's on his way to the club to play tennis. He's heading in the right direction." Piper hopped to her feet and brushed at the grass and twigs sticking to her pant legs. "Maybe he'll come to the snack bar afterward."

"Wouldn't that be great?" Karen suddenly looked down at her clothes. "Oh, no! I look awful!"

"How can you say that when you and I are wearing the exact same thing?" Piper gestured at her white chinos and red polo shirt, the regulation uniform of the Downeast Country Club staff.

"What I meant was, I wish I was wearing something really hot. Or even something normal."

"Yeah, I know what you mean." Piper checked

her watch and picked up her bike. "We have exactly four minutes to get to the club or we may have to turn in these outfits for good."

"Four minutes!" Karen gasped. "We'll never make it!"

"Yes, we will. We'll take the shortcut. Follow me!"

Piper led Karen down a tree-covered alley that snaked downhill behind the mansions. It linked up with other narrow lanes used only by the garbage collectors and delivery men. At a break in the hedge, Piper abruptly angled to the left, and the two cyclists burst out onto a private tennis court, which they crossed in a flash.

Then they were back on the main road, and the wrought-iron gates of the Downeast Country Club loomed in front of them. Only a simple wooden sign, painted red with tiny white initials spelling "D.E.C.C." upon it, announced the club entrance.

When Piper had complained that since the lettering was so tiny, someone could easily miss it, Karen had retorted, "That's the point. If you don't know where the DECC is already, you've got no business looking for it." She pronounced the club initials as one word "deck," like everyone else in Kittery Cove.

The clubhouse itself had a red-and-white awning that arched out over the circular driveway in front of the main door. The building was a rambling Victorian house, with gabled roofs and sweeping verandas.

"Here we are, with one minute to spare!" Piper spun her bike to a clattering stop on a neatly graveled area off to the side of the front door. The brass fittings glowed richly in the shade of the striped awnings. She slipped her front wheel into the nearest bike rack and turned to face her friend.

"Let's go in through the main entrance," Piper urged. "It'll be faster."

Karen nodded her agreement as she tied a red apron around her waist. Piper did the same, tucking a pencil behind her ear. Then they moved briskly up the steps toward the brass door.

"Just a minute!"

They froze in their tracks at the stern command. A thickset man wearing golf slacks with a red blazer stood beside them. Even though it was still early in the day, his face was already glowing with sweat, and he self-consciously dabbed his balding head with a handkerchief.

"Are you the help?" he demanded. The way he said the word *help* sounded like an insult.

The girls exchanged confused glances. "I—I guess we are," Piper stammered. "We waitress at the snack bar."

"Help always enter through the back door." He jerked his thumb toward the side of the building. "Remember that. Help *never* use the Members' Entrance. It's club policy."

"Yes, sir!" Karen hurriedly picked up her bike and raced around the side. Piper followed closely behind her.

"How embarrassing!" Karen hissed. "Who is that guy, anyway?"

"The name tag on his blazer said 'William Wallace, Pro Shop.' " Piper shuddered involuntarily. "I hope he stays there, and we never have to see him again."

"You said it!"

They stepped up to the service entrance, and Piper grasped the handle firmly.

"Well, 'Help,' come on!" She pushed the door open and Karen and Piper stepped into the kitchen of the Deckhouse, the club snack bar that overlooked the tennis courts. Their boss, Chester Hopkins, was already hovering over the big metal grill, wearing his usual white apron and hat. Chester was very short, and with his curly beard he looked like a leprechaun.

"Ayuh, it's going to be a busy one," he said, flipping a sizzling hamburger with practiced ease. "First weekend of July always is."

The air was already filled with the smell of french fries. A tall glass of milk stood ready on the counter for pickup.

"You girls sit tight," Chester instructed. "Jane will give you your table assignments, and whatnot, in a minute."

Piper poured herself a soda and waited by the service counter. Outside, on the patio, patrons of the club were clustered around glass-topped tables, each protected from the sun by its own striped parasol. Chester was right; for the first time since they'd started work, the Deckhouse was crowded. Off in the distance she could see the manicured greens of the golf course and, to the right, the packed red clay of the tennis courts. Without thinking, Piper checked to see if that handsome boy was out there. A sideward glance told her Karen was doing the same thing.

"*Chester!* Where's my moo?" A petite lady with short-cropped black hair feathered neatly around her face slapped her palm against the counter.

"Right in front of you, darlin'," Chester responded amiably. Piper smiled in spite of herself. They all knew that Jane LeBeau's bark was a lot worse than her bite. Her gruff exterior covered a generous heart.

Jane slapped a couple of blank order pads and pencils in front of her two waitresses and looked them squarely in the eye.

"Karen, tables one through five. Piper, six through ten," she said briskly. "I'll cover the rest, and float." Jane clapped her hands and motioned toward the patio. "Come on, girls. Let's hit the Deck!"

Piper hastily gulped down the rest of her soda and headed for the swinging door out of the kitchen. "Piper, do me a favor!" Piper turned to see Jane scoop up the glass of milk from the counter and set it on her tray. "Take this glass of moo out to Mr. Bigelow, okay? Table seven."

"Sure thing," Piper replied and stepped out into the bright sunlight of the patio. An elderly gentleman dressed smartly in a navy blue blazer was sitting at table seven. She smiled cheerfully and set the glass in front of him.

"Here's your milk, Mr. Bigelow. Anything else?"

The old man did not reply but stared intently at the glass. Finally he raised a bony finger.

"Young lady, I always drink my milk from a clear glass," he sniffed. "This one is tinted red."

"I'm sorry, Mr. Bigelow," Piper said smoothly as she reached down to remove the milk. "Would you like me to get you another glass?"

Mr. Bigelow slapped his hand across the top of the glass. "That won't be necessary! Just see that it doesn't happen again!"

"Yes, sir." As she walked back to her station, Piper thought glumly, *This is going to be one of those days.*

Chapter Two

When four o'clock rolled around, Piper was absolutely exhausted. She and Karen had been on the run the entire shift, except for a short break around one-thirty.

By the time the girls had rung off the register and counted their tips, it was almost five o'clock. As they stepped out the back exit of the Deckhouse into the cool outside air, Karen heaved a huge sigh of relief.

"What are you doing tonight?" Piper asked as they ambled across the lawn toward the driveway.

"I'm going to get on my bike and ride it home, slowly. Then I'm going to take a long, hot bath and try not to think about work until tomorrow morning."

"I'm with you!" Piper said, leading them toward the bike rack. They passed a freestanding bulletin board just outside the entrance to the members' lounge. It was plastered with announcements and notices.

"Listen to some of these names!" Piper giggled, pointing to the board. "Leslie Symmons-Smith. Harrison Birney Lloyd the Third. Dexter Horton, Jr.—"

"And they're all looking for tennis partners!" Karen scanned the long list and moaned, "Why didn't I take tennis lessons instead of piano?"

"Oh, Karen!" Piper gasped. "There it is!"

"What?"

"The Harlequin Ball! It's set for July fifteenth! That's less than two weeks away." Piper could hardly contain her excitement. The Harlequin Ball was the jewel in the crown of every summer. For years she and Karen had dreamed of going to it. Last summer, they had canoed across the harbor and watched from the water as the elegantly gowned and masked revelers danced in the ballroom of the country club. The next day she and Karen had spent hours poring over the pictures in the society pages.

"Karen, we have to go this year!"

"You're crazy! In the first place, we could never afford it."

"Where there's a will, there's a way," Piper insisted. "I mean, look how many kids applied to work here last January—and they hired us! That was practically a miracle!"

Karen had to agree. All the local teens, from

Kittery Cove to Bangor, scrambled each year for one of the scarce jobs at the prestigious DECC. Lately more and more applications were coming from students out of state, making the competition even stiffer.

Piper grabbed Karen by the shoulders and looked intently into her friend's eyes. "There *must* have been a reason for it happening to us! Karen, this summer you and I *have* to go to the ball!" Her voice was low and hushed. "We may never have a better chance in our entire lives!"

Karen looked at her friend as if she had lost her mind. Then she grinned and giggled. "Okay!"

"All right! On July fifteenth, we're going to have our hair done!"

"Dress up in beautiful gowns!"

"Arrive in a fancy car!"

"And stay out dancing until two, or three—"

"Or four in the morning!" Piper burst into an impromptu waltz around the bulletin board.

Just then the door of the men's locker room flew open, and two guys in tennis whites stepped out into the light.

"I'll be just a minute, David," the shorter of the two said. "I'll meet you at court three, okay?"

He was David! The tall, tanned vision they'd seen walking that morning by Sea Cliff. Piper felt her heart start to race. He was even more handsome up close. As the shorter player loped toward the office, David trotted off around the corner of the building.

Piper and Karen looked at each other in solemn awe.

"David," Piper whispered. "His name is David!"

Piper stood for a moment, gazing dreamily in the direction he had gone. "What do you think his last name is?" she wondered out loud.

"The Third," Karen replied with a grin. "Isn't everyone's?"

"Let's follow him!" Piper was already moving in that direction.

"Piper, are you kidding?" Karen grabbed her arm. "Mr. Wallace might catch us. We could get fired."

"David is within reach—we can't just let him walk away." Piper pulled a brush out of her pack and ran it quickly through her hair. "Maybe we can introduce ourselves as official employees of the club."

Karen shook her head. "You go ahead, I'm out of it." She moved wearily to her bicycle. "Besides, I'm exhausted. Say hello from both of us."

Piper paused for only a second. She could not believe it. Usually Karen was the one who jumped right into things while she hesitated, considering all the angles. But this was different. She had to meet David!

Piper took a second to look carefully around

to be sure Mr. Wallace wasn't lurking nearby. Then she casually stepped off the patio and strode toward the tennis courts.

"Mr. David Barkley," a voice announced over the public address system, "you have a telephone call."

Piper watched as David set his bag down on a bench by his court, then turned and jogged lightly across the grass toward the clubhouse.

This is it! He'll pass right by me! Piper thought, tugging nervously at her shirt. Her heart pounded in her chest as he came nearer and nearer. She tossed her brown hair, flashed her brightest smile and opened her mouth to speak.

"Ah-oo-gah!" The sound of an old-fashioned horn blared through the air, causing her to freeze in her tracks.

"Oh, no!" she moaned. "Skip!"

Piper turned and watched helplessly as her older brother drove his battered orange Datsun up the gravel driveway. It had big dents in the side and back, earning it the nickname the Orange Crush. He hit the horn again, and Piper winced.

"Hey, Pipes!" Skip stuck his head out the window. "What are you, deaf or something?" His red hair sparkled in the sun as he smiled and waved.

Piper didn't know what to do. There was no

17

place to hide. She was out in the open, and the nearest person to her was David, who had paused to see what all the commotion was about.

When Skip started to open the door and get out, Piper hissed, "Stay where you are! I'm coming." Keeping her head down, she flung the back door wide open and threw herself into the backseat shouting, "Drive!"

Skip obliged and stepped on the gas hard. The Datsun skittered away from the curb with a spray of gravel. Piper lay still on the seat and kept her eyes closed tightly, hoping against hope that David had not seen her.

"Why did you come to get me?" she moaned. "I rode my bike to work. Now I'll have to walk to work tomorrow. And why do you have to honk that awful horn?"

"Hey, Pipes," Skip's voice cut in. "I want you to meet a friend of mine."

"Not now, Skip," Piper said, raising her head up over the backseat to peer out the rear window. There was no sign of David on the lawn. "I don't really feel up to it. And I look awful."

"I think you look just fine," a deep voice answered.

Piper spun so quickly in her seat that she bumped her head against the side panel. A dark-haired boy was grinning at her from the front passenger seat.

"I—I didn't know you were there," she sputtered.

"I guessed that." Amused he raised an eyebrow, then stuck out his hand. "I'm Max. Pleased to meet you."

Piper, still reeling with embarrassment, shook his hand and managed a polite smile. Then she leaned over and punched her brother on the shoulder. "Skip," she whispered hoarsely, "you should have told me someone else was in the car!"

"Why would I have to tell you?" Skip answered, grinning at her in the rearview mirror. "Max is sitting right beside me. If you had just opened your eyes and looked, instead of cowering in the backseat like a—"

"Okay, okay!" Piper interrupted. "You've made your point." She slumped down in the seat and quickly reviewed a number of ways to torture her older brother. First he had humiliated her in front of David, and now in front of this new guy.

Piper peered at Max through lowered lashes. His arms were tanned and muscular, and his black hair had a tousled look, as if he had just run his hand through it. *He must be Skip's age,* she thought, *about eighteen.*

As if he had overheard her thinking about him, Max turned around and leaned an elbow over the back of the seat. "Are you hiding from someone?" His brown eyes flickered with a contagious good humor, and Piper felt herself wanting to smile back at him.

"Actually," Piper answered, lifting her chin to look him in the eye, "I'm devising a plan to do away with my brother."

Max nodded. "I know the feeling. I have two brothers myself." Then he leaned over and whispered, "But any physical harm you do to him now might be dangerous for us all."

He gestured meaningfully at Skip, who was driving and bobbing his head in time to the car radio.

Piper giggled. "You're right! We'll wait until he parks the car, then peel off his freckles, one by one."

"What are you two whispering about?" Skip called over his shoulder.

"That's our secret," Max replied, smiling at Piper. Then he turned around and faced forward.

He has a dimple in his cheek, Piper thought as the Datsun rattled down the road. Then she shook her head vigorously. This was no time to think about Skip's friends. She had bigger fish to catch—specifically, David Barkley.

That night Piper could hardly wait to call Karen. So much had happened in one day! She hurried into the kitchen and poured herself a big glass of milk. Then she sat down at the table and dialed her friend's number.

"Guess what David's last name is?" she blurted out as soon as Karen picked up the receiver. They had known each other so long that they didn't bother saying hello.

"I give up." Karen liked to get to the heart of the matter.

"It's Barkley."

"As in Barkley Bank? Barkley Hill? Barkley University—"

"And Barkley's billions," Piper cut in.

"That is totally awesome."

There was a moment of silence as the enormity of who David really was sank in.

"Karen?" Piper asked. "You still there?"

"Yes. I was just thinking."

"About how rich he is?"

"More like how rich we aren't."

"So?" Piper challenged. "What difference should it make?"

"Well, in case you've forgotten, he belongs to the club and we just work there. That's the difference."

"So? He still needs a date for the Harlequin Ball. Why not one of us?" Piper was not going to let anything dampen her enthusiasm.

"I've been meaning to mention that," Karen said slowly. "You said, 'one of us.' I don't think it's such a great idea for the two of us to go after the same guy."

"Hmm. Maybe you're right." Piper reached for an oatmeal cookie in the jar on the kitchen counter and took a loud, crunchy bite. "That reminds me, Karen. I met a good-looking guy today. I think you might like him."

"Oh, sure, I get it," Karen snorted into the phone. "You're going after David, and I get this 'good-looking' guy. If he's so 'good-looking,' why aren't you interested?"

"Oh, he's just a friend of my brother's. They met out clamming." She quickly changed the subject. "Besides, I saw David first, you know."

"Let me remind you, Piper Elliot, that I saw the hunk first and then handed you the binoculars."

"So?" Piper took another bite of cookie. "I found out all the details about him."

"Details?" Karen's voice was growing louder by the second. "You found out his last name, that's all!"

"What does it matter?" Piper asked soothingly. "Look, if he asks you out first, then I'll back off, and vice versa, okay?"

Karen thought for a moment and answered, "All right." Then she started giggling.

"What's so funny?" Piper asked.

"We haven't even met this guy yet and already we're discussing dates and—"

"You're right," Piper cut in. "We need a plan." She reached for another cookie. "Meet me here tomorrow morning. We'll canoe out to Blueberry Island and think up a good one."

Blueberry Island was where they had always done their important thinking. It was where they had planned their strategy for Piper's successful campaign for student council and also where they had first kissed a boy—Michael Cunningham, in the fourth grade. They had bribed him with baseball cards Piper "borrowed" from Skip's collection.

"I'll pack some submarine sandwiches," Karen said, as always the first to think of food.

"Great!" Piper said.

"Ten o'clock sharp!" Karen ordered, and hung up the receiver. That was another thing that had evolved between them over the years—they never said goodbye.

Chapter Three

"Land ho!" Piper yelled to Karen from the bow of their canoe that Sunday morning. A pair of cormorants, hearing her cry, lifted off the glassy surface of the cove, flapping heavily toward the horizon.

"Blueberry Island!" Karen announced with a grin. She flipped up the bill of her weathered Red Sox cap and dug her paddle deep into the water.

The aluminum canoe scraped up onto the white gravel beach, and Piper, in her faded blue swimsuit, leaped out of the bow. She'd rolled the cuffs of her baggy jeans up, but water still splashed on them as she pulled the canoe onto shore.

Karen clambered out of the stern and tossed her paddle into the canoe. She'd worn a pair of white running shorts pulled up over her old tank suit. On top of that was a bright pink T-shirt.

Together they stowed the canoe out of sight behind some brush above the waterline. Piper adjusted her green visor to shade her nose. Even though it was early in the day, the sun already felt hot on her skin.

"I think this is my most favorite place in all of Maine," Karen said quietly. "Maybe the world."

"Mine, too." Piper turned and smiled at her best friend. "Our secret spot."

The first visit of the summer was always a special event. They stood with their hands on their hips and surveyed the little island.

"Let's be sure to come back here every year," Karen said. "Even after we've gone away to college."

Piper nodded fervently. All at once she felt a little teary eyed. In two months they would be seniors. So much could happen after they graduated and moved away. This summer suddenly seemed more important than any other. She looped her arm over Karen's shoulder and gave her friend a quick hug. Karen hugged her back, her green eyes looking a little misty.

"Come on!" Karen said in a gruff voice. "Let's go see how the old hut held up over the winter."

Karen picked up her pack filled with two hero

sandwiches and a thermos of lemonade and led them toward the little path that cut through the center of the island.

"The undergrowth isn't so bad this year," Piper commented as she forced her way through the woods.

"I wonder if we're the first ones here?" Karen asked, fending off a low branch.

"I would think so," Piper said. "I mean, summer has just started."

"Remember scout training?" Karen giggled. "Maybe we should check the north side of the trees to see if anyone's been there."

Piper laughed out loud. "You've got that all confused! No wonder you and I never got any merit badges."

"Yeah, I think we were the only ones in our troop with completely blank green sashes. There it is!" Karen stepped into the clearing first.

"It's perfect," Piper whispered, coming up beside her. "Nothing has changed."

The girls gazed lovingly at their old clubhouse, a little shack made out of weatherbeaten gray boards. The wood must have been painted white at one time because little chips of paint still clung to the joints of the rafters.

"A little more of the roof has blown away," Piper pointed out. "But the door is still here."

They tugged on the door, and it swung back noisily on its rusty hinges. Peering through the doorway into the living room, Piper could see the rugged Maine coastline framed in the old bay window. Karen and Piper had never known it to have any glass in it.

Piper stepped through the door and moved quickly to the window seat. She dropped her pack on the floor and pulled out her notepad, then sat cross-legged on the seat and smiled at Karen. She felt right at home in their old clubhouse.

"Now," Piper said, pointing to the notepad, "we have to make a list of our goals for this summer."

"Good thinking!" Karen joined her on the window seat, dug into her pack, and pulled out a hero sandwich.

"What are you doing?" Piper demanded. "We just got here."

"If we're going to think, we have to eat." She unwrapped the sandwich and took a big bite. "How do you expect me to be clever on an empty stomach?"

Piper shook her head in disgust. "How do you ever make it through tests at school?"

"I always sneak a little peanut butter and crackers into the classroom." She bit off another hunk of bread and mumbled, "That helps me make it to lunch. After that, I'm good for at least two hours."

Watching Karen devour her sandwich made

Piper hungry. Reluctantly she reached in for her own sandwich, then stared thoughtfully out the window.

"Now let's try to concentrate on our goals."

"Well," Karen said, pulling a piece of cheese from her hero and nibbling at it, "the main thing is the Harlequin Ball."

"I've already put that second on the list."

"Second?" Karen mumbled. "What's first?"

"David, of course." Piper gaped at her friend. "And getting a date with him."

"Oh, yeah," Karen said. "I forgot."

"How could you forget David?" Piper shook her head in disbelief, then leaned back against the window and whispered, "Everything about him is perfect. He's gorgeous, and he belongs to the club."

Piper smiled and took a large bite of her sandwich. She chewed thoughtfully and gazed out the window. There, directly across the water, looking more splendid then ever, was the gray and white mansion.

"Sea Cliff is definitely third." Piper leaned forward to print the words.

"What do you mean?" Karen asked.

"Getting an invitation to it, and seeing inside." They stared across at Sea Cliff. The dormered windows glittered back at them in the sun.

"I mean," Piper said, "we have waited all our

lives to see the inside of that mansion, and now that someone lives there . . ."

"Yeah . . ." Karen breathed.

"Now the question is *how*." Piper tapped the pen to her forehead, then leaned forward and printed, *Find out who lives at Sea Cliff.*

Piper finished her sandwich, wiped the crumbs off her lap, then recapped their agenda.

"Okay, so here it is: We meet David, go to the Harlequin Ball, and then visit Sea Cliff."

"Sounds good to me." Karen clapped her hands together. Then she whispered, "Wouldn't it be wonderful if we *did* do all that?"

"Yeah." Piper hugged her arms around her knees and gazed longingly at Sea Cliff. The French windows had been thrown open to air out the rooms, and freshly painted wicker chairs dotted the lawn. The old house seemed full of life again.

"You remember how we used to think Sea Cliff was haunted?" Karen asked.

"That was because it sat empty for so long," Piper said. "And we were just kids."

"Yeah, we'd never feel that way now." Karen giggled.

"P-i-i-p-e-r!" An eerie moan wafted through the cabin.

The hair on the back of Piper's neck stood straight up. Something was saying her name!

Both girls froze stock-still and listened with all their might.

"P-i-per!" This time the sound seemed farther away, as if it were outside the window.

"Did you hear that?" Piper whispered, not moving a muscle.

Karen nodded slowly, and together they turned to face the window.

"Oh, no!" Piper exclaimed. "I don't believe it!"

"What?" Karen asked.

"It's Skip. He's followed us out here."

"Oh, really?" Karen's face brightened, and she quickly tucked her T-shirt into her shorts.

"Really." Piper watched two figures wave at the island from a wooden skiff. "And he's bringing Max."

"Who's Max?" Karen asked.

"The tall, dark, handsome boy I was telling you about."

"You didn't mention tall, dark, or handsome," Karen said, removing her baseball cap and shoving it into her back pocket. "You just said he was a friend of Skip's."

"They're coming around Gull Rock." Piper stuffed her notepad in the pack and moved to the door. "Quick, let's go stop them."

"Wait a minute, Piper!" Karen scrambled to keep up as they crashed through the brambles down to the beach. "What's wrong with having Skip and his friend along on our picnic?"

"Because," Piper called over her shoulder, "we have important plans to make, remember?"

"Oh." Karen shrugged and added hopefully, "Maybe they can help."

"Give me a break!" Piper burst out onto the beach just as the skiff was rounding the cove.

Chapter Four

"Ahoy!" Max shouted from the bow. He was standing precariously with one foot on the edge of the boat.

"Wow!" Karen gushed. "You're right! He is a hunk."

"I didn't say Max was a hunk," Piper corrected. "I said he was tall, dark, and handsome." She watched the skiff get closer and added, "David is a hunk, remember?"

"Oh, yeah," Karen mumbled.

"Request permission to come ashore!" Max called, cupping his hands around his mouth.

"Permission granted!" Karen quickly answered.

Piper watched the two boys maneuver the skiff into the cove. Max was clad in a pair of white cutoffs, and his open cotton shirt flapped like a flag in the breeze.

"Will one of you give us a hand?" Max shouted

as the little boat clunked loudly against the rocks.

Piper stepped forward and held out her hand. Max clasped it and tried to leap lightly onto shore. The sudden movement made the boat shoot out from under him, and he sprawled forward beside Piper.

"Oomph!" They hit the sandy beach with a thud, and for a moment Piper found herself staring deeply into Max's twinkling brown eyes.

"We've got to stop meeting like this!" he cracked, wiggling his eyebrows like Groucho Marx.

Piper didn't know what to say. She was still a little stunned—partly from the fall, but mostly from being so close to Max.

Looking at his thick dark hair falling loosely over one eyebrow and the dimple in his cheek, she realized that Karen was right. Max was a hunk. He wasn't sleek, like David, but good-looking in a careless, haphazard way.

"Hey, that's some grip you've got!" Max grinned down at her, his dimple becoming even more pronounced. "Knocked me completely off my feet." His eyes were bright with amusement. "Do all the natives on this island greet a stranger so warmly?"

"You shouldn't stand up in a boat, you know," Piper scolded mildly, sitting up. "Who'd you think you were, George Washington crossing the Delaware?"

"Hey, Skip!" Max leaped up and brushed the sand off his shorts. "Is your sister always this strict?"

"Sometimes she's even worse," Skip cracked, reaching into the boat. Then he pulled out an old lunch box decorated with pictures of Fred Flintstone and announced, "I say we make camp here!"

"You can't!" Piper protested. "We were here first."

"What do you mean, we can't?" Skip calmly opened the lunch box and removed some sandwiches. "Is this island your personal property?"

Max scooped up one of the sandwiches and dangled it temptingly in front of Piper's nose. "Perhaps a little bribe might persuade you. We've got freshly made, mouth-watering crab sandwiches!"

"Crabmeat?" Karen blurted out eagerly.

"Karen!" Piper glared at her friend. "Whose side are you on? Remember, we have big plans to make, and besides, we've already— "

"I think this island is big enough for the four of us," Karen cut in before Piper could complete her sentence. Then she sat down beside Skip and said, "I'm starved!"

"Now, tell us about these big plans of yours," Max said, popping the top of a soda can and reaching for a sandwich. "Maybe the wizard, here, and I can help you out."

"They're secret," Piper said quickly, not wanting them to know about her crush on David.

"No, they're not," Karen interjected. "You see, we want to go to the Harlequin Ball at the DECC this summer but we—"

"Why would you want to go to that?" Skip broke in.

"Because every girl should go to a real, live fancy ball," Piper explained dreamily, "at least once in her lifetime."

"I believe those were Cinderella's exact words," Max quipped.

"You guys have no sense of romance!" Piper exclaimed, tossing her shiny brown hair.

" 'Romance'?" Max protested, leaping to his feet. "You call 'romance' getting dressed up in a penguin suit looking like a waiter?"

"And clumping around all night to some orchestra your parents wouldn't even like?" Skip added.

"That's not romance!" Max stated. "That's terminal boredom!"

"It's not like that at all!" Karen argued. "Guys look so handsome in tuxedos, and evening gowns are the most beautiful things in the world!"

"Besides, it's a costume ball," Piper said finally. "Everyone will be dressed up in fabulous disguises."

"Arrgh!" Max and Skip clutched at their throats and fell back onto the sand.

"Oh, you guys just don't understand!" Piper sniffed.

"All I know is," Skip announced, sitting back up, "when I went to the prom with Jennifer Haskell, I felt stupid and embarrassed the whole night. I never want to go through that again!"

"That's because you can't dance!" Piper kidded.

"You can't dance?" Max added, looking impressed. "Neither can I. In fact, I hate dancing. I mean, I wouldn't be caught dead going to a party like that."

"Don't worry," Piper said. "No one is ever going to ask you." She flopped back onto the sand with a big sigh. "No one's ever going to ask us, either."

Piper stared up at the vast expanse of sky above them. She was about to mention David, but something stopped her. She turned her head and looked at Max.

He smiled warmly and asked, "Is it really that important?"

Piper looked into his dark brown eyes and answered simply, "Yes."

"Then what's stopping you from going?"

"You have to be a member of the club," Karen explained, reaching over Skip's shoulder and

36

helping herself to another crabmeat sandwich. "It's written in fine print at the bottom of the announcement."

"So why don't you join?" Max suggested, leaning back on his elbows beside Piper.

"Get serious."

"I am."

"Hate to be a wet blanket," Skip broke in, "but you're forgetting something, Max."

"What?"

"Money," Skip replied. "Remember? Funny little green paper with squiggly lines on it?"

"Hard to get," Karen added, "but easy to lose."

"Oh, right, that!" Max chuckled and scooped up a handful of sand, letting it sift through his fingers. "I just thought they might have different rates for people under eighteen."

"You mean, like at the Y?" Piper jerked herself up on one elbow. "Gee, I never thought of that!"

"Aw, come on, Pipes!" Skip scoffed. "The DECC would never do that!"

"Why not?" She sat up. "We'll never know till we try."

"Even if they do have lower rates," Karen said, pulling an apple out of her pack and taking a bite, "it'll still cost a lot."

"And it will be worth every penny!" Piper crossed her arms and gave Karen her that's-final look. Already her mind was racing ahead to the next day when she would ask to become a junior member of the DECC. She imagined herself flitting from one elegant party to another.

Skip's voice interrupted her daydreaming. "We'd better head back. Looks like some clouds are rolling in."

"Right." Max shoved the remains of their lunch into the metal lunch box. Then he leaped to his feet and shouted, "We'll race you back to the mainland! It's me and Piper against you and Karen." Max grabbed Piper's hand and pulled her to her feet. Before she knew what was happening, they were pounding down the beach to the canoe.

Skip and Karen got the skiff out into the cove first as Max and Piper struggled to free the canoe from the underbrush where the girls had hidden it.

Piper started giggling as they tugged at the canoe. As they finally wrenched it loose, she stumbled backward into Max. Out of breath, Piper turned to apologize. Their faces were so close that she could feel the warmth of his cheek against her skin. Piper froze in confusion, unable to break away.

"Loser buys the lemonade!" Skip's voice called, snapping them both into the present.

They both hurriedly pushed the canoe into the water. "Let's go get 'em, partner!" Max cried as they pushed off.

A few moments later the slender craft moved swiftly out of the cove in hot pursuit of the distant skiff. As they paddled furiously to catch up with Skip and Karen, Piper realized she felt wonderfully alive. What was making her feel so happy?

Maybe it was because suddenly all of her dreams seemed within her grasp. The next day she would become a member of the club, she was sure of it. Already Piper could see herself arriving at the Harlequin Ball on the arm of her own Prince Charming. Why shouldn't he be David Barkley?

Piper laughed and dug her paddle into the water. That day, anything was possible!

Chapter Five

"It costs how much?" Piper stood dumbstruck in the DECC office as the man behind the desk patiently repeated the quoted figure.

"Of course, that's only the summer guest fee," he added. "The regular membership is several times that amount." Shifting his glasses up onto his nose, the man peered at Piper curiously. "Do you have a prospective member in mind?"

"Uh, yes! My cousin—my cousin from Boston!" She dug the toe of her tennis shoe into the plush green carpet.

"You know, then, that prospective members must be nominated by two current members of the club. Then the applicant is screened and voted upon by the membership committee."

"Oh?" Piper said weakly.

"Which meets twice a year, in May and December." He leaned back and pointed to the calendar framed in gold on the wall.

"I see," she said as the last ray of hope dwindled away inside her. Somehow Piper found her voice and murmured, "Well, thank you for your trouble."

The man nodded and turned back to the papers on his mahogany desk. Piper backed out of the office and stumbled toward the brass doors. As she pushed them open and stepped outside, the cool rush of salty air brought a sense of reality back to her senses.

Why does reality have to be so depressing? Piper wondered. There was no way she could become a member! The club dues were higher than she had ever imagined. It seemed the more she wanted to go to the Harlequin Ball, the slimmer her chances became.

It's not fair, she thought, shuffling along the concrete path toward the Deckhouse. She paused by the wooden kiosk covered with club announcements and took a few deep breaths.

"Piper, wait up!" Karen shoved her bike in the rack and trotted up beside her friend. "Well?" Her eyes were bright with expectation. "How did it go?"

"Awful, if you want to know the truth." Piper slumped against the bulletin board. "No, it was worse than awful. Hideous!"

"How much does it cost to join?" Karen asked in a hushed tone.

"Let's just say that if you and I worked here for the next ten years and saved all our tips, we still wouldn't have enough."

Karen whistled and dropped back against the board beside Piper. The two of them were silent for a moment.

"It's too bad Skip and Max couldn't take us," Karen said, sighing wistfully. "Now that would really be fun."

"I can just see the society page the next day," Piper chuckled. "Under the picture, the caption would read in big, bold letters: 'Clam Diggers Escort Waitresses to Harlequin Ball!'"

Karen erupted into giggles at the thought.

"And underneath," Piper went on, "the fine print would read, 'And are promptly escorted out the back door!'"

"It's just as Skip said"—Karen giggled, tapping the announcement with her finger—"you've got to watch the fine print."

Piper laughed, then paused and stared hard at the masked figure and beautiful lettering on the ball announcement. She reread the message discreetly printed in tiny letters at the very bottom of the poster:

MEMBERS ONLY, AND THEIR GUESTS

"Wait a minute!" Piper snapped her fingers. "You may have hit on something. Let's not give up hope yet. There's another way to get to the ball. If we can't go as members, we can sure go as guests of one!"

"Like who?"

"Like—" Piper peered over Karen's shoulder at the tennis notices and read off the names. "Like Jordan, or Sinclair, or Royce, or—"

"Or David Barkley!" Karen finished, her mouth widening into a broad smile. Her brow darkened suddenly. "There is just one, teeny problem."

"What?"

"Getting David, or Jordan, or Sinclair, or Royce to take us."

"Hmmm." Piper circled the kiosk, twisting her shiny brown hair around her finger. After a few moments she declared, "I've got it!"

Karen squinted dubiously at her friend. "This isn't another one of your nutty schemes, is it?"

"No, why?" Piper asked, all innocence.

"You're getting that gleam in your eye again. That means *I'm* the one who's going to wind up making a complete fool of myself. I just know it!"

"Karen! How can you say such a thing? Didn't I plan for us to work here and didn't it all work out?"

"Well, yes," Karen admitted. "But last Halloween you also planned for us to win the best costume award—"

"And we won, didn't we?" Piper interrupted, putting her hands on her hips.

"Piper, it took *two* days for the mustache glue to wear off my upper lip!"

"You know how awful I felt about that!" Piper wrapped a sympathetic arm around her friend's shoulder, and the two of them walked toward the Deckhouse. "This idea is much better!" she whispered excitedly. "And it doesn't involve any mustaches."

"Tennis, anyone?" Piper sang out as she stepped into the Deckhouse kitchen on Thursday. She had spent the entire week searching for just the right outfit—a sleeveless white linen blouse with crisp sailor collar and matching short pleated skirt. Piper had even splurged and had her initials monogrammed on the tiny pocket on the skirt.

"Well, what do you think?" Piper flung her tennis racket over her shoulder and struck a jaunty pose by the grill.

"Don't you look just swell!" Chester said, peering around the stove. He grinned and added, "I didn't know you played tennis."

"I don't. I'm just pretending," Piper whispered.

"It's all part of the Big Plan to meet the Right Boy!"

"I don't get it," Chester said.

"You see, I just carry the racket around until some guy—preferably David Barkley—stops me and asks if I want to play."

"But then wouldn't you have to know how to play?" Chester asked, completely bewildered.

"No." Piper giggled. "You see, by the time I've made my moves, he will have completely forgotten about tennis—and I'll have a date to the ball!"

"Sounds too complicated for me!" Chester shook his head.

The slatted door swung open, and a booming voice interrupted them.

"Spuds and suds!" Jane dumped her empty tray on the counter and expertly poured out two foaming glasses of root beer.

"Coming right up!" Chester shouted, tossing a fresh batch of potatoes into the deep fryer.

"Hey, Piper, you look like a real pro!" Jane said as she reached for two straws. "How's the Great Date Search coming?"

"So far—not so good." Piper pulled a piece of notebook paper out of her tennis skirt. "I've met Royce and Tyler, and they're really wimps. I absolutely tower over both of them."

Jane leaned in over Piper's shoulder and scrutinized her list. Piper had put bold check marks next to the names of members she had met and rejected.

"What about him?" Jane pointed to the bottom line of the page. "Milton Artemus Cavanaugh the Third?"

"How could anyone in all seriousness walk around with a name like that?" Karen asked, coming through the swinging door from the patio and joining them. She had started her shift an hour before Piper was scheduled to come on and was dressed in her standard red shirt and white chinos.

"I don't know, but he's one of the few I haven't run into yet." Piper grabbed a bag of potato chips and hopped up on the stool behind the counter. "As I see it," she continued, "all the really handsome guys already have girlfriends, and the rest don't seem to be interested."

"Hey, what about me?" Chester protested. "I'm interested."

"Sorry, Chester, you're out of the running," Jane called back over her shoulder. "The girls are looking for club members only."

"So what else is new?" Chester flipped two burgers without even looking.

"Well, there's still David," Karen said hopefully.

Piper nodded confidently. "That's who I'm counting on."

Jane reached over and stuck her hand into Piper's bag of chips. "Who's David?"

"There!" Karen exclaimed. "That's him." She pointed toward a boy walking across the lawn to the tennis courts. "The vision in white."

Piper caught her breath in spite of herself. As usual, David looked stunning. He moved with an easy athletic grace, expertly flipping his racket up into the air and catching it as it fell. He never dropped it.

A reverential hush came over the two girls as they watched David. Finally Piper broke the silence.

"His name is David Barkley." She sighed.

"Well, good luck," Jane said.

"We'll need it. We can't even get close enough to meet him," Karen grumbled. "He never seems to need a tennis partner, and he hasn't come by the Deckhouse once."

"You'd think he'd get thirsty," Piper complained. "With all the tennis he plays!"

"Karen!" Chester called, interrupting their laughter. "Order up!"

"My feet are already killing me," Karen moaned.

"Help is on the way," Piper promised. "After a slight detour to the tennis courts, that is." She looked at the orders piling up on the counter. "Tell you what," she offered, "I'll take one out with me."

Piper brimmed with confidence as she pushed open the swinging door out to the patio. It was a perfect opportunity to casually run into David. After delivering the tray, Piper intended to saunter by the courts and catch David's eye and maybe talk to him.

As Piper neared the table, she recognized Whitney Poole and Morgan Taylor, two of the most popular teenagers in the club. They were sitting with two other girls. "So we'll all meet at the Grotto Saturday night for dinner, right?" Morgan was saying.

Instinctively, Piper paused a few feet away to eavesdrop. The Lobster Grotto was the most elegant restaurant along the waterfront in North Harbor, with a reputation for having the best seafood in Maine.

"Then we'll press on to Getty's," Whitney added. "Heart Attack is supposed to be playing." Piper knew that Getty's was the "in" hangout and regularly flew in the hottest rock groups from Boston and around the country. Of course, Piper had never been inside, but she would have given her right arm for the chance.

"It'll be fabulous," Morgan added. "And everyone will be there!" She lowered her voice dramatically. "Even David Barkley. Royce Dowling told me he was definitely going."

There was a chorus of giggles, and one of the new girls demanded, "He hasn't asked anyone to the Harlequin Ball yet, has he?"

"Not yet," Whitney replied, then added with a sly grin, "but I'm working on him."

A shiver went down Piper's back. Now it was more important than ever to talk to David. Time was running out.

"I'm starved." Morgan's voice interrupted Piper's thoughts. "Where's the food?"

"Here's your order," Piper said quickly, stepping forward and placing the tray on the table. "Sorry it's late. Need anything else?"

"We're all set, thanks," Whitney answered. Then she noticed Piper's sleek tennis gear. "Hey, that's a cute outfit. Did the club issue new uniforms?"

"No, it's mine. I just got here early, and Karen needed a hand."

"I didn't know you played tennis," Morgan said, raising a skeptical eyebrow.

"Yes, of course," Piper said with a laugh. She couldn't possibly admit to them that she'd bought the outfit just to get a date. Then, before she could stop herself, she added, "I have a tennis game scheduled on court three."

Piper almost bit her tongue off, trying to take back her words. Hurriedly she tried to repair the damage. "Looks like my partner's a no-show," she added ruefully. "Otherwise I'd be playing right now."

"I think he's arrived," Morgan observed, pointing over to the courts.

Piper turned and barely stifled a gasp. There,

to her horror, was David Barkley, limbering up on court three.

"You're playing with David?" Whitney asked. A definite edge of admiration had crept into her voice.

"Sure," Piper replied casually, playing her advantage for all it was worth. "We scheduled it weeks ago."

"Maybe Morgan and I will come and watch you play."

"Fine. Why not?" Piper hoped her voice sounded enthusiastic enough, because inside she felt ill. How was she going to bluff her way out of this?

"You'd better go or you'll be late." Morgan gestured toward the court.

"Oh, yeah!" Piper giggled, a little too loudly. "I wouldn't want to keep David waiting!"

Piper turned and faced the courts. Swallowing hard, she stepped off the patio onto the grass and moved slowly toward David and certain humiliation.

How am I ever going to get out of this? a voice screamed inside of her. *I've never played tennis in my life! Maybe I could just turn around and go the other way.*

Piper quickly checked over her shoulder to see if Whitney was watching her. She was. Piper flashed a big smile, waved gaily, and turned back toward the courts.

Then her mind came up with the only possible way out. She would trip and pretend to sprain her ankle. *I may have to spend the rest of the summer faking a limp,* Piper thought grimly, *but it will be worth it!*

As she approached the chain-link fence surrounding the tennis courts, Piper took a deep breath and mentally prepared herself for her fall.

Before she could start her stumble, a booming voice from behind stopped her cold.

"What do you think you're doing here?"

Piper spun around and nearly fainted. There, as big as life, was Mr. Wallace, the creepy man from the pro shop. His bald head glistened under the afternoon sun, and his beady gray eyes were fixed like daggers on her.

"I, uh, well—" Piper couldn't think of an excuse. All she knew was that this was it! She was going to get fired, right here, in front of Whitney and Morgan and, worst of all, in front of David Barkley.

David had stopped his warm-up exercises and was looking over at them curiously. Impulsively Piper lifted her hand and waved at him. He smiled and waved back. A rush of hope surged through Piper, and she turned back to Mr. Wallace.

"I—I wanted to see if Mr. Barkley left this racket at the Deckhouse," she said quietly, hoping her voice wouldn't carry too far.

Mr. Wallace eyed her dubiously, then took the racket out of her hands and examined it. He spun it around and around in his hands.

"Something wrong?" a deep voice murmured from behind her shoulder. Piper knew without looking up that the voice belonged to David. He was standing right beside her, a concerned frown on his face.

"Oh, hello, Mr. Barkley." Mr. Wallace sounded like a completely different person from his usual blustering self. "This young lady seems to think this racket might be one of yours."

"Really?" David said, taking the racket and twirling it. His hands were tanned and muscular. Piper found herself staring at the perfect little crescent moons at the base of his fingernails.

"It was left at one of the tables at the Deckhouse," she said quickly.

"Looks brand-new," David commented, handing it back to her. "But it's not mine. I gave up wooden rackets long ago."

"Maybe it belongs to one of the younger members," Mr. Wallace said. "I'll take it over to Lost and Found and see if anyone claims it."

Piper watched in relief as Mr. Wallace walked away with her racket. She didn't mind his taking it away from her. It was a cheap price to pay for a chance to be alone with David Barkley.

"I'm sorry to have bothered you," she said

shyly. "I just wanted to be sure you hadn't lost it."

David chuckled and ran his hand through his blond hair. "Oh, it's no trouble at all."

"Miss Elliot!" The bark was back in Mr. Wallace's voice, and Piper's back stiffened at the sound. "I'd like to speak to you a minute, please."

Piper looked up at David and mustered her gamest grin. "Got to run! 'Bye!"

David waved and turned back toward court three. Piper swallowed hard and reluctantly joined Mr. Wallace. *Oh, no*, she thought, *don't let my luck dry up now!*

"This still doesn't explain what you're doing in the members' area out of uniform." Mr. Wallace glared at her sternly and checked his watch. "I don't have time to discuss it now. Consider this a warning!"

"Thank you, Mr. Wallace," Piper managed to blurt out, grateful that he wasn't going to make a scene. "It won't happen again, I promise!"

He buttoned the red blazer up over his belly. "It had better not," he warned. "If it does, you're out of here!"

Piper watched him waddle across the lawn with her tennis racket and held back the urge to stick out her tongue at his retreating backside.

Instead, she marched briskly toward the kitchen. As she passed Morgan and Whitney, Piper brazenly announced, "Got to run! We had a little crisis in the kitchen." She could tell by their openmouthed expressions that they had not overheard a thing. "David took a rain check on the game!"

Once she was safely inside the kitchen, Piper collapsed against the familiar walls with relief.

"I will never, ever tell a lie again," she vowed. "That was too close for comfort!"

Chapter Six

Saturday Piper was riding her bike to work along the coast road when Skip's battered car came up beside her.

"Hey, Pipes, want a ride?" The roar of the broken muffler nearly drowned out Skip's voice.

"Thanks," Piper yelled, "but I'd rather bike it!" Riding her bicycle gave her some time by herself—time to prepare herself for work and clear her mind. These past few days Piper had needed all the mental clarity she could muster.

"Need I point out that you missed your turn?" Skip shouted. "It'll take you fifteen minutes more this way."

"That's okay. I like the route better. It's more scenic." Piper chose not to mention that she had planned to pass by Sea Cliff on her way. Lately it had become part of her regular route.

"Suit yourself!" The old car lurched forward

down the road and stopped. "Hey," Skip shouted out the window, "is Karen scheduled to work this afternoon?"

"Yeah, we're both on the same shift today." Piper pulled her bike alongside the Datsun and peered inside. "Why?"

"Just curious." Skip checked his red hair in the mirror and grinned. "Maybe Max and I will drop by at quitting time, and we can all go do something."

"Karen and I were planning to go to Getty's tonight." She patted her bag, which had her red jersey dress in it.

"Getty's?" Skip raised his eyebrows in surprise. "Why? Who's playing?"

"Heart Attack. I hear they're really hot." Piper didn't mention that going to Getty's was now the last gasp of their Big Plan. It would cost an arm and a leg to get in, but Piper was getting desperate. David would be there, and she knew this might be her last chance to talk to him before Whitney turned on the charm.

"Hey, I've been wanting to hear them. Why don't we go with you!" Skip patted the dashboard of the car. "I'll drive."

"That'd be great!" Piper had wondered how she and Karen would get there. It was a long way around the bay to North Harbor.

"We'll pick you up after work."

"Be sure to use the back entrance when you

come to pick us up," Piper warned. "You know how strict they are about nonmembers." After the warning Mr. Wallace had given her, Piper knew she was treading on thin ice around the DECC.

"No problem. They'll never know we were there!" Skip shifted into gear and sped off down the road. Piper winced as the engine backfired with a deafening noise just before the bend. As the Datsun disappeared around the turn, Skip leaned on the horn and a bleating "Ah—OO-gah!" assaulted her ears.

"Great," Piper moaned as she coasted down the hill. "That car is about as subtle as a sledgehammer."

In a few minutes the gray and white gabled roofs of Sea Cliff appeared above the massive oaks lining the road. Gliding past the hedge, Piper could hear music and voices wafting through the air from the lawn inside. Immediately she felt an irresistible urge to see what was going on. Then she hesitated.

"You're too old to be spying," a little voice inside her warned. But another voice whispered, "David Barkley might be there."

At the thought of David, Piper tucked her bike behind a tree and slipped up the delivery road toward the back of the mansion. She checked her watch and muttered, "Half an hour. I've got time."

Piper could hear voices laughing and talking above the music. She walked along the big sculpted hedge until she found herself directly behind the gray and white gazebo on the back lawn.

Now what do I do? Piper thought. The hedge was thick and looked impenetrable. Then she found a narrow opening and, crawling on her hands and knees, managed to inch her way inside. When she pulled apart the thick foliage for a peek, Piper nearly gasped out loud.

From her hiding place, Piper could see all the way across the dark green grass to the rear of the mansion. The tall French doors had been thrown open from inside, and dozens of elegantly dressed people were standing in little clusters, chatting gaily and balancing plates in their hands. Long tables had been set up at each corner of the lawn, shaded by striped awnings and laden with sumptuous platters of food. Each table had a beautiful flower arrangement for a centerpiece. Nearby, white-coated waiters, their shiny brass buttons glistening in the sunshine, moved discreetly through the party, refilling empty glasses. Piper realized the music was coming from a trio of musicians who sat in the gazebo.

Scanning the crowd, Piper immediately recognized the dapper figure of Mr. Elton Sinclair, the president of the DECC. In fact, it seemed as though half the regular membership of the country club was present. A familiar voice sailed over the others to her ears.

"You see, Mrs. Cavanaugh, I insist on drinking my lemonade from a clear glass, or not at all. It's a matter of principle!"

Mr. Bigelow! Piper chuckled softly. The frail old man was explaining his eccentricities to an attractive older woman dressed in a pale chiffon dress and broad straw hat. The woman seemed less than enthralled by his lecture; Piper was glad to see that he gave everyone a hard time, not just hired help.

Piper was still chuckling when a familiar voice made her catch her breath and listen closely. Two people had circled away from the party to talk secretly behind the gazebo.

"I have my dress but no date!" she heard Whitney say. Piper pushed deeper into the scratchy hedge.

"My mother offered to talk to the Barkleys, and I told her that would be embarrassing," Whitney moaned. "But time is running out!"

"Barkley!" Piper repeated under her breath. She strained to catch every word.

"Whitney," Morgan's voice said quietly, "why do you insist on going to the Harlequin Ball with David? You know Tyler would love to escort you."

"Tyler Harrison is such a baby!" Whitney replied.

"Well, why don't you talk to David yourself?"

"I couldn't do that! It would be too awful. I mean, David hardly notices me as it is."

Piper's eyes widened, then she smiled. So, she wasn't the only girl having trouble getting David Barkley's attention. More important, now she knew David was still available.

Just then two strong hands grabbed Piper from behind and yanked her out of the hedge.

"Help!" Piper yelped, as she was buffeted and scratched by the branches. She twisted around to confront the security guard she was sure had caught her.

Her captor was none other than Max, kneeling beside her with a wide grin on his face.

"You?" she hissed. "How dare you—" Piper clapped her hand over her mouth in horror as she remembered she was still in hiding. She motioned for Max to stay silent and held her breath.

"Did you hear something?" Morgan's voice carried clearly through the hedge. "I thought I heard someone call for help."

"Probably Tyler down by the water, playing one of his practical jokes," Whitney replied in a bored tone. "Let's join the others, okay?"

Piper didn't move a muscle until she was sure the two girls had left the gazebo and gone back to the lawn party. Then she turned to face Max.

"What's the idea of sneaking up on me?" she demanded. "You scared me half to death!"

"I was only trying to help!" Max held up his hands in mock defense. "I saw you squirming around on your hands and knees and figured you'd gotten your head stuck in the hedge."

"Oh, sure!" Piper rolled her eyes at him. "A likely story."

"Then what, may I ask, were you doing in there?"

"I was just—just peeking," Piper said.

"You mean spying." The grin on Max's face was growing wider and wider.

"Peeking," Piper insisted. "I wanted to see what one of these fancy garden parties looked like."

His brown eyes searched her face intently. Finally he whispered, "And what *do* they look like?"

"See for yourself," Piper said, pointing to the opening in the hedge. "But don't let anyone spot you. The place is probably crawling with guards who'll arrest us in a minute."

"I'll keep an eye out," Max promised.

They crawled forward into the tight space on their hands and knees, their shoulders touching, and peered out the other side at the lawn party.

"See?" Piper whispered, her eyes bright with awe. "Isn't it fabulous?"

Max shrugged. "Looks like any backyard barbecue. A lot of people standing around, eating and talking."

"But everyone is so elegant and beautiful. Oh, look, look!" Piper pointed to a tall, blond woman in a long white dress passing by the gazebo. "She could have stepped right out of a painting."

Suddenly Piper realized that she was doing all the oohing and ahing. Max had not said a word. She turned and looked directly into his dark brown eyes.

"What do you suppose people talk about at these parties?" she asked.

"I'm sure they talk about the same things as the rest of us."

"Oh. Do you really think so?"

"You sound disappointed." Max reached up and pulled a twig out of her hair.

"I guess I am," Piper murmured. "It's just that I hoped that people who live in beautiful houses and look so wonderful would talk about wonderful things."

Just then, two plump ladies in big straw hats, flowered sundresses and white gloves, circled the gazebo, and Max and Piper ducked back into their hiding place.

"I can't eat raw fruit any more," the one was saying to the other. "It gives me indigestion."

"I'm that way with radishes," the other responded.

Piper and Max looked at each other and tried hard not to explode with laughter.

When the ladies passed out of sight, Max

cracked, "That's about the most 'wonderful' conversation I've ever heard!"

Piper began giggling uncontrollably. Max joined her, and the two laughed until tears rolled down their cheeks.

Finally Piper sighed. "I guess I just didn't want them to be—ordinary." She thought about it for a moment and added, "And I don't want to be ordinary, either."

"That's one thing you don't have to worry about," Max said huskily. He smiled then, and Piper couldn't tell if he was teasing.

Piper was suddenly aware of how close Max was to her. His face was only inches away, and the spot where his shoulder touched hers felt hot, as if it were burning. For a moment Piper enjoyed the closeness, but then, embarrassed, she backed quickly out of the hedge into the lane and sat up, rubbing her knees.

Max followed suit and the two sat quietly for a moment, staring at each other. The music from the party stopped, and there was a smattering of polite applause.

"So, uh . . ." Piper tucked her hair behind her ear. "Skip said you guys would take us to Getty's tonight."

"Getty's?"

"Yeah, a lot of the kids from the DECC are going to the Lobster Grotto and then on to Getty's. Since we can't do both, we decided to catch the group at Getty's."

"Why can't we do both?"

"Too expensive."

"If I said it was my treat," Max asked, "would you go?"

"Sure I would!" Piper exclaimed. "Are you kidding?"

"I'm not kidding, Piper." Max's voice was low and serious. "If you want to go, I'll take you. I mean it."

Piper hesitated. "What about Karen and Skip?"

"I'll treat them, too." He slipped the sunglasses onto his nose and wiggled his eyebrows. "I've had a great week working in the clam business."

"Work!" Piper checked her watch and knew the worst. "Oh, no! I'm going to be late. Come on! Let's go!"

"Why do we have to go?"

"I have to get to work, and you can't just hang around here. What if they see you? You'd get thrown into jail for loitering, or vagrancy, or worse!" Piper grabbed him by the arm and pulled him away from the hedge. "Keep your head down," she whispered.

"It's a free country," Max grumbled as he stumbled along beside her.

"That's what you think!"

When they reached her bike, Max picked it up off the ground and held it steady for her.

"Karen and I will meet you guys at the Deckhouse this evening," Piper said excitedly, hopping onto her bike. "Oh, I can't wait! Don't be late, okay?"

"Sure thing, boss!" Max replied, swinging up onto a limb of the big oak tree by the front gate. He dangled by his legs upside down as she pedaled off. "See you later!"

At the bend, Piper turned around to wave and watched Max neatly dismount from the limb with a flip and twist. He landed on the grass with the practiced ease of a gymnast, shot Piper a big grin and a wave, and disappeared up the service road behind the trees.

I wonder if David Barkley would ever do anything like that, Piper marveled at Max's antics. She shook her head at the thought and chuckled. It was hard to imagine David with his hair mussed up.

"David!" A sudden realization struck her, so forcefully that Piper abruptly braked to a stop. "He wasn't at the party at all! And I didn't even notice!"

Chapter Seven

"Drop us off here!" Piper leaned forward and tapped her brother on the shoulder.

"But the Lobster Grotto's still a block away!" Skip answered, looking at her in the cracked rearview mirror.

"I know, but we want to make a good impression. And, well . . ." Piper paused, trying to think of a tactful way to say that Skip's car was a wreck and she was embarrassed to be seen in it. "Maybe walking up to the door would make a grander entrance," she ventured hopefully.

Skip slammed on the brakes, and the car screeched to a halt. "Either the Orange Crush takes you to the front door, or you get out here—forever!"

Piper winced. She should have known better than to criticize Skip's dilapidated pride and joy. When it came to his car, Skip had no sense of humor.

"I vote for the front door," Karen sang out from the front seat.

"Seconded by me!" Max added as he silently motioned for Piper to go along. Piper realized that Skip was not going to budge.

"Then the front door it is!" Piper made her voice sound cheery and light. The prospect of walking all the way back to Kittery Cove outweighed any embarrassment derived from arriving in the Orange Crush.

Skip hit the accelerator and maneuvered the car smoothly up to the curb in front of the Lobster Grotto's outdoor patio. "Ladies," he announced, "we are definitely here!"

As Karen got out of the front seat, Max leaped out the rear door and vaulted across the trunk to Piper's side. He swung her door open with a flourish, bowing low as she stepped onto the curb.

"Will madam be wanting anything else?" he intoned starchily.

"That will be all, James," Piper quipped. "You and Skippy may park the Rolls in back."

"Veddy good, mum." Max dipped low again, slammed the door, and then hopped onto the front hood of the car. Skip beeped the horn, and the car edged toward the parking lot with Max posed like an ornament on the hood.

The people dining outside had stopped talking and were gaping at the new arrivals.

"Well, we can either turn around and never come back to this restaurant again," Piper whispered out of the side of her mouth, "or we can go with the flow."

Karen took another glance at the crowd, then nodded her head. "Let's go with the flow. Something tells me this isn't going to be any ordinary Saturday night."

Piper made a grand gesture of offering her arm to Karen. "Shall we?"

The two paraded across the patio to the entrance, pausing just long enough to blow kisses to the crowd before disappearing into the restaurant.

They stepped through the door, and Piper froze. There, not ten feet from her, was David Barkley!

He was dressed completely in white—pleated linen pants, canvas suspenders, a soft cotton shirt, and canvas loafers. He was perfectly casual, yet elegant. Everything about him looked pressed. Even his hair.

"Hi, David!" Piper called out cheerily.

David nodded pleasantly, but it was obvious he didn't have the slightest idea who she was. Piper felt the blood rush to her face as she explained, "We're from the club."

"Oh?" He still couldn't place them.

"We work there," Karen blurted out.

"We're waitresses at the Deckhouse," Piper explained even further.

"Oh! I see." A glimmer of recognition flickered across his face. "Sorry. I didn't recognize you."

"Yeah, I can understand," Karen cracked. "We look so different out of uniform."

"That must be it." Either David had completely missed the sarcasm in her voice, or he was choosing to ignore it. David pointed to a short, stocky guy standing beside him. "This is Royce Dowling."

Piper recognized him as one of David's regular tennis partners at the club. Everyone smiled politely, but Piper felt her cheeks burn with embarrassment.

"Well, it was nice meeting you," David and Royce chorused mechanically as they followed the waiter to their table.

Piper collapsed heavily onto a bench by the wall. "That was so embarrassing," she whispered. "He acted as if he'd never seen us before!" She shook her head, completely flabbergasted. "I mean, we work there every day! Boy, do I feel like an idiot."

"He's the one who should feel like an idiot," Karen snapped. "Mr. Observant. Well, he's off my list."

"Mine, too," Piper agreed, crossing her arms—but she didn't really mean it.

"Besides," Karen added, pointing toward the far side of the restaurant, "It looks as if Whitney has dibs on him."

Whitney and Morgan were sitting in the corner, looking poised and beautiful. Piper watched as David briefly stopped to talk to them. "I wouldn't be so sure about that. David didn't recognize us, but he doesn't look that thrilled to see her, either."

"At least we've got dates that want to be with us, and aren't a couple of sticks-in-the-mud," Karen muttered.

"Yeah, you're right."

At that moment Skip and Max sauntered into the restaurant. Karen turned and graced them with a dazzling smile.

"Skip! Max!" Karen threw open her arms. "Where have you been? We missed you!"

Skip and Max stopped dead in their tracks, then quickly looked behind them. Their startled faces provoked hoots of laughter from the girls, who took their arms and led them toward the dining room.

"Four for dinner?" A middle-aged man clad in a dinner jacket and bow tie greeted them at the door.

"We have reservations," Max said, pointing to the list on the podium. The man nodded and then smiled brilliantly. "Of course! With a view of the harbor. This way, please."

He gestured for them to follow him and began to thread his way through the tables toward the window.

Moments later they were all seated at what had to be the best spot in the restaurant. Their table looked out through the large plate-glass windows revealing the twinkling lights of North Harbor. The moon was almost full, and the yachts in the bay were clearly visible, rocking at their moorings. Far off in the distance the light-house at Schooner Point blinked on and off like a metronome.

"Pretty slick move," Piper whispered to Max as they sat down.

"It pays to call ahead." He shot her a confident wink, then turned his attention to the waiter, who was handing out the menus. "That's all right. We'll all be having the lobster special— and for an appetizer, bring us two plates of steamed mussels and clams, with plenty of garlic butter and french bread."

"Certainly, sir." The waiter slipped away with the order.

Piper, Skip, and Karen sat in their places, looking a little stunned.

"Max?" Piper broke the silence. "Are you sure you can afford all of this?"

"No problem!" He grinned at them like the cat

who ate the canary. "I checked the price list on the board outside the restaurant." He leaned back in his chair and lifted his glass to his friends. "Relax and enjoy your delightful dinner, courtesy of the fertile clam beds of the State of Maine!"

An hour later the table was piled high with dishes filled with discarded bits of lobster and mussel shells. As the waiter cleared the mess away, the four diners leaned back in their chairs, completely sated. It had been a fabulous dinner.

"I think the most fun part about eating lobster," Karen said giggling, "is seeing your guys wear those silly bibs."

"Well, you look pretty silly in yours, too," Skip pointed out good-naturedly and nudged Karen with his elbow. This made her giggle even more.

All of them were wearing big plastic bibs with pictures of dancing red lobsters on the front.

"I think I'll keep mine," Max said, "as a souvenir of this perfect evening." He smiled at Piper as he took his off and carefully folded it up. Then he tucked it away in his pocket.

Piper felt herself blush at his smile, and she quickly changed the subject. "But the night has just begun! We still have dancing at Getty's."

"I can't wait," Karen gushed. "I hear Heart Attack is really a great band!"

"I can't believe I agreed to go dancing," Skip

said, shaking his head sadly. His face looked so mournful that Piper had to stop herself from laughing.

"Waiter!" Max waved as their server passed by on his way to the kitchen. "Check, please!" The waiter nodded and within seconds presented the bill on a salver in front of Max.

"This is really great of you to treat us," Piper said, as Max studied the bill.

"No kidding!" Skip stood up and pushed his chair under the table. "We'll do the same for you sometime."

Max wasn't listening. He was digging into his pockets—methodically checking the back pockets first, then the front ones. The pockets of his jacket came next and finally the breast pocket of his yellow oxford-cloth shirt. The others watched him repeat this routine several times.

"Did you lose something, Max?" Piper asked. She glanced over at the waiter, who was waiting patiently beside Max, balancing the bill on the salver.

Max looked up at them and smiled feebly. "You're not going to believe this," he said, bending over to check under the table, "but I seem to have lost my wallet."

"Oh, no! Max, that's awful!" Piper whispered as she helped him look.

"Maybe I left it in my other pants," Max said, shaking his head.

The waiter did not bat an eyelash. He turned and immediately handed the bill to Skip, who passed it over to Piper like a hot potato.

"I can't believe this is happening," Piper muttered, looking from Max to Skip and back again. She set the bill down on the table and rummaged through her purse. Her hands were shaking with embarrassment as she tried to count her money. Finally Piper said, "All right, everybody, put what you've got on the table."

One by one they emptied their pockets onto the white, linen tablecloth.

By this time, the room had gone quiet as everyone in the restaurant turned to stare at them. Piper just knew that their humiliation was being witnessed by Whitney, Morgan and, worst of all, David Barkley. She wanted to sink into the floor.

"Here's the money for my ticket to Getty's." Karen pulled two ten-dollar bills from her back pocket and dropped them on the table. "That's all I've got."

"Me, too," Skip murmured, adding his to the pile. "Plus some loose change."

Piper looked over at Max. "Well?" she asked.

He held his empty palms up in mute reply.

She turned back to the bill. "Fortunately, I brought some extra money. So that should just cover it." She glanced over at Karen and mumbled, "Except for the tip."

Karen groaned audibly.

"Wait a minute," Max said, reaching into his front pocket. The others looked at him hopefully. He sheepishly pulled out a quarter and set it on the pile.

Piper found another dollar bill tucked away in the bottom of her purse and shoved it all into the waiter's hand. Without saying another word, she turned and marched straight for the door. The others followed suit.

No one said anything until they had reached the car. Piper slumped against the door and moaned, "That was awful. I never dreamed I could feel so humiliated."

Karen nodded her head in agreement. They were all still in shock. Skip stood silently by the front bumper, thumping the tire with his foot.

Piper looked over at Max. He was standing off to one side, still staring back at the brightly lit facade of the restaurant. His face looked pale and drawn. "Max?" she asked. "Are you okay?"

He shook his head. "I'm sorry, guys," he said. His voice seemed flat and empty. "Really sorry." Then Max turned and looked over at Piper. "I owe you one. All of you."

"Forget it," Skip said kindly. "It could've happened to any of us."

Max shook his head stubbornly. "I can't forget it. And I won't."

"What do we do now?" Karen asked. "It's eight o'clock on a Saturday night—"

"And we're flat broke," Piper finished. She sighed heavily and stared down at the concrete. "Maybe we're just not meant to do special things," she muttered.

"What do you mean?" Skip asked.

"I don't know," Piper replied. "Maybe the wonderful things you read about in books only happen in books. Or to other people. Lucky people. I don't know. . . ."

"Well, Getty's is certainly out of the question now," Karen said. Then her voice cracked slightly as she added, "And I really wanted to go, too!"

"Wait a minute!" Max stepped in front of the mournful trio and demanded, "What's preventing us from having a great time tonight?"

"Money," Skip retorted. "How else are we going to get into Getty's?"

"Forget Getty's!" Max waved his hand impatiently, then stopped himself. A funny look came over his face. "I'm truly sorry about all of this," he began, "but, what if I showed you how to have a blast without spending a penny? Would you be interested?"

"How?" All three chorused in disbelief.

Max took a deep breath. "All we need is gas in the car—"

"That, we have," Skip said.

"And some empty suitcases."

"Suitcases?" Piper looked up at him in confusion. "What on earth for?"

"Trust me!" Max opened the back door of Skip's Datsun. They stared at him dubiously, without moving. "Please!"

"Oh, what the heck," Karen said, turning to Skip. "What have we got to lose?"

Skip grinned suddenly and jumped into the driver's seat. Karen scrambled into the passenger side.

"Piper?" Max looked at her hopefully, that mischievous twinkle back in his eye. Piper grinned back, curious to see what he had in mind, then scooted into the backseat.

Max jumped in beside her and shut the door. His arm brushed hers lightly, and Piper felt a tingle of warmth at his touch. Without thinking, she started to move close to him, then stopped herself.

Here they had just been humiliated in front of an entire restaurant of people, David didn't even know her name, the Harlequin Ball was now just a dream—and all she could think about was resting her head on Max's shoulder.

She peered over at Max through lowered lashes. What was it about him that affected her that way?

Max turned to look at her and suddenly winked. "Don't look so worried," he said confidently. "You're going to love this!"

"I'm not worried—" Piper started to reply, then let her voice drop off to silence. She looked out the window and tried to collect her thoughts. Things were happening awfully fast, and it was all very confusing.

Skip started the engine. As he revved the motor Karen hung over the seat back and asked, "Where to, maestro?"

"To the Elliot house first." Max turned to Piper and explained, "For the suitcases. And then—to the airport!"

"Airport?" Piper shouted as Skip swerved out of the parking lot and headed for the highway. "Max, have you completely lost your mind?"

Chapter Eight

An hour and a half later Piper and Karen stood at the entrance to Concourse B of the Bangor International Airport, clutching their suitcases and looking slightly bewildered.

"I can't believe we're actually doing this." Karen giggled, readjusting her sunglasses for the fifth time.

"Me, either!" Piper pulled the brim of her purple felt hat down low over her eyes and looked nervously at the people milling around them. "And I hope no one we know recognizes us in these getups!"

When Max had described his plan for the evening in the car, all three had rejected it outright. Even Skip, who was usually game for anything, thought the idea was too weird.

The game was called Hail and Farewell! The

idea, as Max explained it, was pure simplicity—the girls would join the crowd of arrivals from an incoming flight, and the guys would pretend to be their husbands coming to meet them.

"Imagine that you and your partner have been separated for a long, long time," Max had suggested. "It could be for all sorts of reasons. Maybe you got split up in Paris during the war—"

"Like Humphrey Bogart and Ingrid Bergman in *Casablanca*!" Karen enthused, getting into the spirit. "Oh, that's so romantic!"

"Right!" Max said. "Or you were a prisoner in Siberia—"

"And a campaign, led by your famous poet-husband," Skip said, "has forced them to finally let you rejoin your family in the West!"

"You've got it!" Max grinned like a proud parent as Skip and Karen made up one outlandish scenario after another. The Datsun sputtered over the highway toward the airport.

"I guess I only have one question about this game," Piper said. "Why would *anyone* in their right mind want to look so silly in front of dozens of strangers?"

"For the *fun* of it!" Max said, his eyes dancing mischievously. "And it's free."

Piper laughed out loud. The expression on Max's face was irresistible.

As soon as they had reached the airport, the

quartet checked the schedule board, agreed on a flight, and split up to wait its arrival.

"Now, what did Max say we were supposed to do?" Karen whispered nervously.

"When the flight arrives, we back into the crowd. Remember to pretend like you've just gotten off the plane."

"And then the guys will meet us."

"Right." Piper could see Max and Skip pretending to look at newspapers by the gift shop at the end of the corridor. Skip was wearing Mr. Elliot's trench coat and gray slouch hat. Obviously he had decided to be a spy. Max was wearing a sports cap and sunglasses, with the collar of his jean jacket flipped up like James Dean.

"Flight four fifty-one has just arrived," Piper announced, glancing up at the television screen above their heads. "It's at gate four. Ready?"

"I'm as ready as I'll ever be!" Karen picked up the brown leather suitcase beside her and shifted it to her left hand. She had stuffed Skip's catcher's mitt in it to give it some weight.

The two girls moved quickly down the corridor toward the gate where people were already streaming out toward the baggage claim. They melted easily into the rush of arrivals.

"I hope Ralph remembered to come and meet us," Karen said in an nasal voice. "He's *always* late."

Piper turned to gape at her friend. It was just like Karen to dive in. Piper, stifling the giggles, decided to play along.

"My husband, Leonard, is just the same," Piper clucked, making a big deal of checking her watch. "I hope he managed to find a baby-sitter for the kids."

"How many children do you have now?" Karen lowered her glasses to the tip of her nose.

"Five," Piper said, without batting an eye.

Karen made a noise that sounded like a goose honk. Then she started coughing so loudly that a couple of people who were walking near them paused to whisper to each other.

"Of course, they're not all mine," Piper continued, blithely ignoring the onlookers' curious stares. "Four of them are from his first two marriages."

Karen was still gasping for breath and wiping her eyes when they turned the corner by the gift shop. Max and Skip were engrossed in their newspapers and hadn't seen the girls yet.

"Oh, look!" Karen squealed, pointing at Skip. "It's my Ralphie—and he's on time!"

Karen, flinging her arms wide and still clutching the suitcase, ran in slow motion toward him.

Skip hesitated for only a second. Then he ran toward her as well, taking huge leaps and bounds through the air.

Upon seeing Piper, Max tossed the paper over his shoulder, whipped off his sunglasses, and shouted dramatically, "Charlotte, my darling! You've come back to me!"

"Oh, Leonard!" Piper grabbed her purple hat and tossed it in the air. "I've missed you!"

They ran joyfully toward each other. When Piper was a few feet from Max, she dropped her suitcase and leaped into his arms. Max caught her and spun her around in a circle.

As soon as he set her down, Piper asked, "Leonard, how are the children?"

He threw back his head and laughed. "They're wonderful!"

"All five of them?"

The corner of Max's right eye twitched just slightly. Then he held her at arm's length and cried, "But, Charlotte, didn't you know?"

"Know what?" she asked, all innocence.

"We've had two more!"

"That's fabulous!" Piper threw her arms around Max's neck. He caught her around the waist and hugged her, his cheek pressed close to hers.

Then it happened, so quickly that it was over before Piper could react. His arms tightened around her waist, and their lips met in a kiss. Piper felt a charge of electricity surge through her body.

She pulled back to catch her breath, her deep

brown eyes wide with astonishment. Max, his arms still around her, looked as surprised as Piper. His luminous brown eyes searched hers for one brief moment as they stood frozen in each other's arms.

Then Skip's voice broke the silence.

"I didn't bring you any flowers, Agnes, because I didn't think of it!"

"Sure, Ralph, you never think of anything," Karen screeched back at him. "I have half a mind to get right back on that plane!"

"I have half a mind to put you on it," he retorted. "Then I'd have some peace and quiet around here!"

Karen faced him defiantly, her hands on her hips. "I dare you!"

Skip bent forward, threw Karen over his shoulder, and carried her kicking back toward the gate. Karen hit him with her suitcase, and it fell open, the lone baseball glove falling onto the floor with a plop.

Skip and Karen exploded with laughter and crumpled to the floor. Piper giggled as she watched the two of them try to get the suitcase shut again. Max chuckled beside her.

"Piper?" he asked in a quiet voice.

"Yes?" She looked up at him, still feeling a little wobbly from the kiss.

When their eyes met, he started to stammer, "I—uh, I'd—"

"Yes?" she prodded gently.

"Your—your hat is on the floor." Max pointed to the purple hat she had thrown into the air. It lay in the middle of the corridor and at least one pair of feet had stomped on it.

Piper went to retrieve it with her insides feeling the way the hat looked—squashed.

She reminded herself that she, Piper Elliot, was not supposed to be interested in Max—strange, handsome, mysterious Max. She had her heart set on David Barkley.

"Hey, it looks like it's just us chickens," Skip said from behind her. Piper looked around and realized the corridor was deserted. With a start she also couldn't help noticing that Karen and her brother were holding hands—and it wasn't make-believe anymore.

"That was a total hoot!" Karen's voice bubbled with delight. "What do you say we try a different concourse next?"

"Yeah," Skip agreed, "I think they've folded up shop here."

Piper looked over at Max, who was staring out the huge glass windows of the concourse, his lean frame silhouetted against the dark night sky. Beams from incoming planes and landing lights flickered across his face.

Abruptly Max turned away from the window and flashed them all a dazzling smile. "Let's go up to the observation deck!" he suggested. "No trip to an airport is complete without it."

A few minutes later they were greeted by the high-pitched whine of jet engines as they pushed open the glass doors onto the roof of the terminal. The wind was blowing so strongly, Piper felt herself blown against Max as they struggled toward the railing.

Instinctively Max put his arm around her shoulder to steady her. The four of them huddled by the rail, staring out at the blue lights lining the runway.

A jet began its takeoff and rumbled past them with a roar, finally lumbering up into the sky. They watched its blinking lights fade into the darkness as the roar turned to a low rumble and then was gone.

"There's something kind of sad about airports," Piper said. "Especially at night. They seem so lonely."

"Where'd that come from?" Skip asked.

"I don't know. Every time a plane takes off, someone goes away and someone is left behind. That's sad." Piper shook her head. "I guess it makes me think how, at the end of this summer, nothing will be the same." She looked up at Skip and said, "You'll go off to college and only come back to visit on holidays."

"Yeah, but I'll write you tons of letters. And

I'll call you a lot." Skip grinned and added, "Collect."

"Karen and I will be seniors this year," Piper continued, "and pretty soon we'll be going away, too."

"But we'll always be friends." Karen reached over and squeezed Piper's arm. "Forever."

Another jet emerged from the dark horizon and settled down onto the runway. The squeal of its tires hitting the pavement seemed unusually loud in the cool night air.

"What about you, Max?" Piper asked suddenly. "What are you going to do next year?"

"I'd really like to travel," he said, "before I go to college." He pulled his jean jacket closer around him and buttoned the two lower buttons. "That's why I like airports. To me, every time a plane takes off, it means a new adventure is about to begin for someone."

"I've never looked at it that way," Skip said. "But you're right."

"I still think airports are sad," Piper said wistfully, "because the planes come and go, and we're not part of the adventure."

"What do you mean?" Skip protested. "The Datsun is in the parking lot ready and waiting for takeoff."

"Yeah." Max chuckled. "Just riding in that car is an adventure in itself."

Piper stared out at the forlorn ribbon of runway, stretching away to nothing. Abruptly she shivered.

"Are you cold?" Max asked.

Piper nodded, and he gently put his arm around her shoulder.

"I wish we could get on one of those jet planes tonight," she murmured, "and disappear forever! Or at least until next Friday is over."

"What's on Friday?"

"The Harlequin Ball, silly!" Piper lightly jabbed him with her elbow.

"Oh, right!" Max said. "How could I forget?"

"I don't think I'd mind being left out of it so much," Piper added wistfully, "if I were somewhere else that night."

"You still really want to go to that, don't you?" Max asked.

Piper nodded. "Oh, I know it's silly, and the people who are going to be there are silly, too, but . . ." She shrugged. "I still want to go."

"Me, too," Karen said quietly.

"Then you'll go," Max said. His lips seemed to brush the top of her hair.

Piper didn't move. "What do you mean?" she whispered.

"If it means that much to you, I'll take you." Then he spoke in a louder voice to Skip, "In fact, I think we should all go!"

"What? Crash the biggest event of the social season?" Skip chortled with disbelief.

"Why not?" Max asked.

"We'd never get away with it," Skip replied.

"And Piper and I would get fired for sure," Karen added.

"Why would you want to go to a ball, anyway?" Skip demanded. "I thought you hated those things."

"Maybe I've had a change of heart," Max responded.

"The question is—how are you going to get us into a ball that is strictly for members only?" Karen asked. "I mean, let's face it, Max, you can't even get us out of a restaurant!'

"I said I was sorry about that!" Max replied. "But, in a funny way, I'm glad it happened." He lightly squeezed Piper's shoulder. "If I hadn't lost my wallet, none of this would have happened tonight."

"I guess it's fate." Karen giggled. She and Skip were standing together in the darkness a little distance away.

"Besides, where there's a will, there's always a way." Max's voice had a new, firmer edge to it. Then he whispered into Piper's ear, "Right, Cinderella?"

Piper closed her eyes and bobbed her head slightly. She hadn't uttered a word during the entire exchange. In fact, she'd hardly breathed. Funny things were happening to her. She felt light-headed, and calm, and warm, and shivery, all at once. It was all very confusing.

The only thing Piper was sure of was that she believed Max. She believed him with all her heart. Why, she had no idea. It was not reasonable; it was not logical. She just knew that—somehow, some way—next Friday evening, she, Piper Elliot, would be going to the Harlequin Ball!

Chapter Nine

"Look at this haircut," Karen said, barely moving her lips. She turned stiffly and held up a picture from one of the fashion magazines.

It was late Wednesday evening, and both girls had covered their faces with an oatmeal-and-water facial. It was part of their beautification plan. They were trying hard not to move their mouths or their masks would crack.

"How do you think I'd look in it?" Karen asked.

"Your face is too square, and that cut would only emphasize it," Piper said, keeping her face just as rigid. "I like your curls just the way they are."

"What do you mean, my face is square?" Karen hopped up and walked slowly to the mirror in the Elliots' living room. "I think my face is oval."

According to the magazines they'd been reading, oval was the perfect shape and any other was almost a handicap.

"Actually," Piper observed, "it's hard to tell when it's covered in oatmeal."

"How long do we have to keep this stuff on?" Karen reached up and carefully scratched her nose.

"Until it's completely dry and forms a hard mask."

"Great!" Karen moaned. "What if my face sticks this way for good?"

Piper tried hard not to giggle, but she couldn't help it. Little chunks of oatmeal dropped onto her lap as her face creased into a smile.

"I'm serious!" Karen said. "Then it won't matter what my hair looks like."

Piper had narrowed her own choices for hairdos down to three and had them laid out on the floor in front of her.

"It is so hard deciding on just the right look for the ball." Piper sighed. "I wonder how socialites do it, week after week."

"Well, I bet they don't get their ideas from magazines," Karen said, still studying her face in the mirror.

"Yeah, they probably just walk to their closets, reach in, and *violà!*—it's the perfect outfit."

"Speaking of outfits . . ." Karen frowned at her reflection. "Did you know that Morgan and

Whitney are flying down to Boston tomorrow for their final costume fittings?"

"It must be nice to be wealthy." Piper tossed another magazine onto the pile beside her.

"You know, Piper, I hate to say this," Karen said, "but I'm a little worried about letting Max arrange for our dresses."

"Well, you and I didn't have any luck finding a costume-rental store," Piper said, coming to his defense.

"I know, I know," Karen admitted. "Even the stores in Bangor were all booked up."

"Max said he knew of just the perfect, inexpensive place—"

"That's just it," Karen cut in. "I mean, you don't think he'd take us to a thrift shop or someplace like that for our gowns, do you?"

"Gosh, I hope not." Horrifying visions of faded, old Halloween costumes ran through Piper's mind as she rose to her feet. "I mean, he *knows* it's a fancy dress ball, right?"

"Right," Karen echoed weakly. "And we know how much he likes the idea of dressing up in fancy clothes."

"He wouldn't!" Piper started pacing back and forth, nearly slipping on the fashion magazines. "He knows how much this means to us!"

"Maybe we should call him," Karen suggested nervously. "Just to make sure."

"You're right. Let's do it now." Piper marched

right to the kitchen phone, picked up the receiver, pointed her finger at the buttons, and stopped.

"What's the matter?" Karen asked.

"I don't know his number," Piper said, replacing the receiver on the hook.

"Well, Skip must have it written down somewhere." Karen handed Piper the Elliot family's beat-up address book.

"Yeah." Piper opened the cover, and a dozen slips of paper fell out, fluttering to the carpet. In fact, the book was crammed with scraps of paper, envelopes, and even a couple of napkins, all with names and numbers written on them.

"Karen?" Piper looked up. "What is Max's last name?"

"I don't know." Karen scratched her head. "I don't think I've ever heard it."

"Oh, he must have told us," Piper said, anxiously flipping through the address book. "We just don't remember."

"No." Karen shook her head. "I think I would have remembered it. I have a good memory for names."

Piper slammed the book shut and tossed it back on the cluttered counter. "We'll just go to his house and tell him."

"Where does he live?" Karen asked.

"I was afraid you'd ask that." Piper slumped

against the wall. "Karen, this is really weird. I mean, we don't know a thing about this guy."

"Oh, you're just being overly dramatic!" Karen chastened. "I'm sure Skip knows all about Max. We'll ask him when he comes home."

"Okay." Piper tried to sound enthusiastic, but a little warning bell was going off inside her head. "Don't you think it's odd," Piper asked, trying to keep calm, "that we haven't seen Max since the airport? That was days ago!"

"No," Karen said flatly. She opened the refrigerator and examined the contents. "I mean, we've been really busy at work, and so has he." She pulled out an apple. "Is it okay if I eat this? I can't think on an empty stomach."

"Sure, go ahead," Piper said absentmindedly. "I mean, he *did* say he would take us, and all that, right?"

"Right." Karen crunched into the apple. "And we all believed him."

"Right!" Piper tried to recapture the feeling she had had on the observation deck with Max so close beside her. She had been so certain about him then—so certain that she had even given up trying to get to know David Barkley.

"I guess I'm just being silly," Piper said, moving back to the living room. "Must be nerves."

Karen took another bite of her apple and mumbled, "Now you've made me nervous. Why hasn't he called?"

The back door suddenly slammed, and they heard Skip's voice call out, "Hello? Anybody home?"

"Piper, hide me!" Karen whispered, trying to duck behind the sofa. "Help!"

"Karen, it's only Skip!" Piper pulled her friend up by the arm. "What are you worried about?"

"Hello?" Skip called again. They heard the refrigerator door open and shut.

"We're in the living room," Piper yelled.

"How could you!" Karen mouthed, little bits of oatmeal flaking onto the floor. Then she covered her face and ran for the front door.

"I thought I heard another voice," Skip said as he entered the living room. "Who else is here?" He was busy trying to stuff a handful of chocolate-chip cookies into his mouth.

"Karen *was* here," Piper replied. "But she just left."

Skip took a big swallow of milk from the carton he was holding and nearly choked. "What happened to your face? It looks like it melted!"

"Nothing happened," Piper retorted, putting her hands on her hips. "This is an oatmeal mask."

"Well, I hope you're not planning on walking around on the street like that!"

"No, dummy!" Piper moved to the mirror and carefully patted her face. "It's done," she announced primly, "and I'm going into the bath-room to wash it off."

As she headed out of the living room, she nearly collided head-on with Karen, who was coming in from the other side.

"Oh! Hi, Skip," Karen said with exaggerated surprise. "When did you get home?"

Piper stared at Karen's flushed face and grinned. Karen must have used the garden hose to wash off the mask, then dried her face with her T-shirt. The wet smudges along the bottom of her shirt gave her away.

Karen's green eyes widened dangerously as she gave Piper an if-you-say-anything-I'll-strangle-you look.

Piper shrugged and turned back to her brother. "By the way, Skip, Karen and I just realized that we don't know Max's last name."

"We thought you would know," Karen said.

Skip started to take another swig of milk, then stopped. "You know," he chuckled, a puz-zled look on his face, "I don't know it, either."

"Well, you must know where he lives," Piper insisted.

"Nope." Skip shook his head. "We always meet at the beach, or down on the docks." He looked at their dismayed faces and asked, "Why?"

"Because, dear brother," Piper said slowly, trying to contain her anxiety, "the ball is two days away, and we haven't heard a peep out of him."

"He's supposed to find a place for us to get all of our costumes," Karen added in a choked voice.

"And get us in!" Piper and Karen stared expectantly at Skip.

"Gosh, you guys, I don't know what to tell you except"—Skip looked from one to the other and shrugged—"be patient."

Chapter Ten

Shortly after dawn on Friday morning, Piper stared at her reflection in the bathroom mirror. She hadn't slept well at all. In fact, for the past two days Piper had tossed and turned in sleepless torment every night.

"I look awful!" she moaned, convinced that purple rings were developing under her eyes. As she reached for her brush to untangle her matted hair, she noticed she had bitten the nails on her right hand all the way down to the quick. It had taken two months to grow them!

"That does it!" Piper declared, slamming the brush down on the sink. "I've got to call Karen. Now!"

Piper marched into the kitchen and squinted up at the wall clock. It was still only seven in the morning. She debated for a second, then picked up the phone and dialed.

"This is an emergency!" she muttered under her breath.

After six rings, there was a click on the other end and a groggy voice answered, "Hello?"

"Still no word from that jerk!" Piper announced.

"Piper?" the voice croaked. "Wha-what time is it?"

"It's seven in the morning," Piper answered. "The ball is exactly thirteen hours away."

She stared numbly at the date circled in red on her calendar, and it blurred as her eyes filled with tears.

"Hasn't Skip been able to find him yet?" Karen asked.

"No. He's out at the beach right now, looking. Mom even took Skip's paper route this morning so he could drive around early."

"Wow."

"And even if we do find him, it's too late to get a costume." Piper angrily rubbed her eyes with the back of her hand, fighting back tears. "I hope Skip *does* find him. I've got a few thousand things I want to say!"

"Boy, he sure took us for a ride." Karen's bitter laugh rang hollowly on the line.

"Yeah, starting with pretending to lose his wallet at the Grotto," Piper said.

"You think he did that on purpose?" Karen gasped.

"Of course! He couldn't have paid for it!" Her

voice shook with fury. "He was just trying to show off."

"Gosh—" The line fell silent. Then Karen asked, "You don't think he ever intended to take us to the ball?"

"Of course not! That was just part of his little scheme." Piper's voice was scornful and cold. "You didn't really believe he could get us in, did you?"

"Well, yes," Karen admitted. "Didn't you?"

"No! Never!" Piper heard her own voice ring shrilly in her ears. "I knew it was just another one of his practical jokes."

Karen's voice seemed to come from far away. "I was really looking forward to going with Skip. . . ."

"Yeah, what is it with you and Skip, anyway?" Piper demanded.

"Wha—why are you being such a grouch?"

"I'm not being a grouch! It's just that, he's *my* brother, and I think it's really weird, if you want to know, that you two are getting so chummy all of a sudden."

"I happen to like Skip, and he likes me!" Karen snapped. "What's wrong with that?"

Piper suddenly felt bad. "Oh, I'm sorry, Karen, I don't know what I'm saying." She slumped against the kitchen counter. "I guess I feel really stupid for letting Max make such a fool of me."

"Well, if it makes you feel any better, he made fools of all of us."

The memory of the kiss in the airport swam into Piper's mind. How could she have blown one little kiss so far out of proportion? She had trusted him, trusted him completely. Her face burned just thinking about it.

"The worst thing is, I can't even yell at him," Piper fumed. "I can't believe that we don't know his last name, or where he lives, or his phone number, or anything!"

"I guess I assumed Skip knew all that," Karen said.

"Don't you think it's strange we never went to his house? He probably lives with a bunch of crooks!" Piper let her imagination run rampant as she paced back and forth across the kitchen floor, yanking the telephone cord behind her. "He's part of a big crime ring. They travel around the country taking advantage of poor, unsuspecting girls!"

"Piper," Karen interrupted, "we never go to my house, either. But that doesn't mean I'm a crook."

"*You* don't go around getting people to fall in love with you, and then disappear without a trace—" Piper clapped her hand over her mouth in horror.

"What did I hear you say?" Karen whispered into the telephone.

102

Piper sank weakly onto the kitchen stool. "I don't know why I said that," she muttered, shaking her head. "I'm upset, I'm not myself—"

"Maybe you *are* in love with him," Karen broke in. "Which would explain why you're so upset."

"That's ridiculous!" Piper rasped into the phone. "In love with that jerk? Never! I just want to go to the ball, that's all!'

"Hey!" Skip's voice sounded from behind her. "What's all the shouting about?"

"Listen, Karen," Piper said, looking at her brother, "I'll see you at work. Here's Skip." She thrust the receiver into his hand and threw open the back door. She needed some fresh air.

I'll be fine, she thought, taking a deep breath, *if I can just make it through this day!*

At ten minutes to eleven that morning, Piper and Karen swung their bikes into the circular drive of the Downeast Country Club, but they weren't looking forward to work. The drive was bustling with activity as they pedaled up to the club. Several vans were lined up by the service entrance, and Mr. Wallace, a clipboard in his hand, was shouting instructions to the delivery men. The shiny dome of his bald head glistened in the sun.

Extravagantly beautiful floral arrangements, all in purple and orange, were being carried through the back entrance into the grand ballroom.

"That's Bird of Paradise," Karen gasped. "There must be two hundred of them in those arrangements!"

"There couldn't be that many in all of Maine," Piper marveled. "I'll bet they flew them in from Boston, or maybe New York!"

They watched, openmouthed, as an elaborate floral arch was carefully lifted out of the back of the florist's van and carried into the building.

"That must be for the entrance to the ballroom," Piper whispered.

Three more trucks pulled up to the back door as Karen and Piper were locking their bikes. Crates of fresh fruits and cheese, platters of cakes and pastries, and other delicacies were carted through the back door in what seemed like a never-ending line.

"Amazing, isn't it?" Chester commented, stepping up beside them in his white apron and chewing on his trusty pipe.

"Chester, it's awesome!" Piper gushed. "Is all of this for the ball tonight?"

"Ayuh," Chester grunted. "Pierre St. Juste arrived bright and early this morning on the red-eye from Boston. But as yet, I haven't had a chance to meet him."

"Who's Pierre?" Karen asked. "Sounds like a poodle."

"For your information, Pierre St. Juste is only the greatest chef on the whole Eastern Seaboard of these United States."

"Why, Chester," Piper exclaimed, "I didn't know you cared about those things."

"I don't intend to sling hash all my life," Chester huffed indignantly. "I'm a pretty darn good cook—when I'm given a chance." He took his pipe out of his mouth and whispered conspiratorially, "In fact, Jane and I have been talking about opening our own little restaurant, and whatnot."

"You and Jane?" Karen raised a cautious eyebrow, unsure how to interpret this new information. "You mean, like partners?"

Chester nodded vigorously. "It's still a secret," he confessed. "Though I guess I've let the cat out of the bag." Every line on his face crinkled with pleasure.

Karen and Piper ran for the kitchen door, squealing with delight, and cornered Jane by the pantry. As Chester came into the kitchen behind them, Jane shot him a warning look.

"Nothing I could do about it, Janie," he said. "They forced it out of me."

As Piper prepared the patio tables for the day, she mused about how funny it was that Jane and Chester had gotten together. They seemed so different. Chester was like a cuddly toy, easy-

105

going and unflappable, whereas Jane was sharp-edged and sassy.

The more Piper thought about it, the more it made sense. They balanced each other and made a great team.

Thinking about couples made Piper depressed. Jane had Chester, it looked as if Karen had Skip, but Piper had no one.

Why hadn't Max called her? Where was he? Why had he just disappeared like that, after making her feel that there might be something special between them?

"Oh, no!" Karen moaned, coming up beside Piper and interrupting her thoughts. "Look who just sat down at table ten."

Piper looked up to see Mr. Bigelow settling into the red-and-white striped chair. "He must be the only person not going to the ball."

She and Karen looked around at the empty tables. By eleven-thirty, the Deckhouse was usually full, but not that day.

"Excuse me, miss," Mr. Bigelow said, raising one finger and pointing at Piper. "I would like milk, in a clear glass—"

"Paging Cinderella!" the intercom suddenly blared. Piper recognized Jane's voice over the speaker. "Paging Cinderella!"

"Excuse me, Mr. Bigelow," Piper said excitedly, "but I think I hear my fairy godmother calling."

"Fairy godmother?" the old gentleman exclaimed.

"If I'm right," Piper added with a smile, "you can have your milk in a rainbow glass for the rest of the summer." She tried to thread her way calmly through the tables, but by the time she reached the kitchen door, she was at a dead run.

"Where is he?" Piper gasped, bursting into the kitchen. Chester and Jane looked up calmly from the counter, receipts and bills strewn in front of them.

"He, who?" Jane asked.

"He, who, Max!" Piper shrieked.

"I didn't see a Max," Chester answered, then turned to Jane. "Did you?"

Jane shook her head.

"Then what was that message—?"

"Oh, wait a minute!" Jane interrupted. "A delivery boy came to the back door a few minutes ago. He told us to page a 'Cinderella,' and then to give whoever answered the call this note."

Jane held up a little pink envelope with a gold seal on the outside. Piper's hands were trembling as she tore it open and read the printed message inside:

Humbly request the pleasure of your company, along with Skip and Karen, at the Harlequin Ball tonight at eight o'clock.

Prince Charming

P.S. Remember, your house 8 P.M. SHARP!

Piper hugged the note to her chest and deliriously hopped around the kitchen. Then she stopped and asked, "What did this delivery boy look like?"

"Well, let me see," Chester rumbled, scratching his chin. "He was about six feet tall—not a bad-looking fellow—dark haired—"

"Was his hair combed?"

"No," Jane replied. "It looked pretty rumpled. Very attractive, though."

"That's Max!" Piper shouted triumphantly.

"What's going on?" Karen asked, pushing through the swinging door and dropping her empty tray on the counter.

Piper smothered her with a ferocious hug. "He's taking us to the ball!"

"Who is?" Karen demanded, trying to untangle herself from Piper's arms.

"Max is, that's who!" Piper squealed. "Just as he said he would!"

Karen grabbed Piper's hands, and the two jumped up and down in sheer delight.

"Oh, no!" Karen said abruptly.

"What's the matter?" Piper asked.

"We don't have any costumes!"

Before Piper could absorb this new development, she heard Chester drawl from the corner, "Well, maybe there's something in this old leather trunk here." He gestured to a battered steamer trunk sitting by the hall door. It had huge, brass buckles and the words "Acadia Summer Theater" stenciled on the side.

"That's what the delivery boy delivered," Chester explained.

Karen and Piper moved slowly toward the trunk. Piper unclasped the buckles and slowly lifted the lid with both hands. Timidly she took a peek inside.

"They're costumes!" Piper gasped.

"And they're beautiful!" Karen added, throwing back the lid and lifting up a blue velvet bodice with satin ribbons.

Before the girls could pull any more costumes out of the trunk, Jane stepped forward and slammed the lid shut.

"Just a minute! You can't do that here," she commanded. "This is a place of business, not a dressing room!"

Piper and Karen looked up, dismayed by the sternness in her voice.

"But, Jane," Piper protested weakly, "these are for the ball!"

"That's what I figured. Chester," Jane ordered brusquely, "take this trunk out back, put it in the pickup and drive it over to the Elliot house."

Piper and Karen stood numbly as Chester bent over and began dragging the trunk into the hall.

"You'd better go with him," Jane added casually. "I'm giving you the day off. This place is like a ghost town."

The girls leaped to hug her, but Jane brushed them off good-naturedly.

"I'd quit wasting time if I were you," Jane added, a warm gleam in her eyes. "You've got a ball to go to!"

Chapter Eleven

"Oh, Piper, is it really, *really* us?" Karen whispered, her voice low and hushed as the two girls stood before the big mirror in the Elliot living room. They stared in wonder at their reflections as the old grandfather clock in the hall slowly chimed the hour—eight o'clock.

"We look like little porcelain dolls," Piper murmured, adjusting her velvet choker. Piper was dressed as Columbine, the beautiful heroine from the traditional Italian pantomime. She had seen the play last year at the Acadia Summer Theater, and remembered admiring the dress then. But who would have ever guessed she'd actually get to wear something so beautiful?

That's just like Max, Piper thought to herself, *to go to a real theater company for real costumes!*

Her ankle-length white dress was hand-painted

silk and chiffon, with layers of petticoats underneath. Over that, a blue velvet bodice that laced up with gold cords made her waist seem tiny. Delicate ballet slippers tied at the ankles with blue and pink ribbons that matched the designs on her skirt.

Karen, dressed to look like Little Bo Peep in pale blue and yellow, looked as if she had stepped out of a storybook. Little white lace bloomers peeked out from under her hem, and a few of her own blond curls tumbled out from under the straw hat with a big blue bow that tied under her chin.

"Good evening, ladies!" Skip appeared in the doorway and bowed with a flourish. He was disguised as one of the Three Musketeers. Big leather boots, laced cuffs, and a plumed hat made him look almost dashing. He'd drawn on a goatee, and with his black mask it was hard to recognize him.

"Oh, Skip," Karen gasped. "I never would have guessed it was you!"

"Me, either," Piper admitted. "And I'm your sister!"

"That's the idea!" Skip chuckled and handed them both their masks. "Remember, the note Max included with the costumes said to be sure to wear these!"

The three of them posed in front of the mirror

some more. Karen adjusted Skip's collar several times, insisting that it was on crooked.

"I know this sounds silly," Piper said as she twirled around once more before the mirror, "but I *do* feel like Cinderella!"

"And tonight you get to join Morgan and Whitney at the ball." Karen giggled. "Won't they be surprised!"

"Oh, Karen, we can't tell!" Piper warned. "Max specifically said we had to keep our identities secret."

"Do you think he meant it?" Karen fluffed up the material in her sleeves. "Or was he just saying that to make all this seem more mysterious?"

"I'm not sure," Piper admitted. "But, just to be on the safe side, we'd better take his word for it. After all, he's the one who's going to get us in. He must have a plan."

A loud honking and ringing of bells erupted from the lawn outside. Skip ran to the window to investigate.

"Cinderella," he yelled back into the room, "I think your coach has arrived!"

Piper skipped to the door, visions of elegant chauffeured limousines dancing in her head.

When she reached the door, Piper had to squeeze her eyes shut, and open them again, to be certain that what she was seeing was real.

There, in the Elliots' driveway, was the oddest contraption she had ever seen. It was completely covered with brightly colored ribbons.

"It's—it's a—" Piper stammered.

"It's a bicycle built for two!" Karen clapped her hands together with delight.

"For four," Skip corrected. "And not one of them is the same kind of bike!"

Piper realized that some enterprising inventor had thrown together the frames of four different bicycles and welded them into one. An old-fashioned Schwinn, a touring bike, a racer, another with huge balloon tires—each was painted a different bright color, with multicolored streamers woven through the spokes. And on each set of handlebars was attached a different kind of horn.

"Welcome aboard the quadricycle!" Max shouted from his perch on the lead bicycle. Then he leaped off and sprinted up the walk to the door. Piper took a good look at his costume and gasped.

Max had chosen to go disguised as Harlequin himself, the namesake of the ball. With a shiver of delight Piper realized that Harlequin was the character in the play who fell madly in love with Columbine. Max's costume was a collection of bright red and blue triangles, patched onto tight-fitting breeches and an elegant short jacket. He wore a black hat that looked as if it had been borrowed from Napoleon.

114

"He looks fantastic—as though it were made for him!" Piper whispered to Karen.

As Skip and Karen ran down to the street to inspect the bicycle, Max came up to Piper on the porch.

"You look beautiful!" His voice was low and fervent, and Piper suddenly felt shy.

"Thank you," she said, feeling the blush rise in her cheeks. "The costumes are incredible, Max. Where did you—"

He raised his hand and interrupted. "No time to explain. I'm just glad they worked out. What do you think of my quadricycle?"

"I think it's terrific!"

Max gestured for her to take the place behind him. Karen scooped up her skirts and hopped on behind Piper. Skip brought up the rear.

"Now, this is a little tricky, but with a little bit of practice, I think we'll have it down," Max said, as they struggled to back out onto the road. He tooted his horn and waved his hat in the air. "Forward, ho!"

Two false starts and one near collision with a fire hydrant later, the foursome wobbly made their way toward the club. They reached the top of the hill by the overlook without any further incident.

"I know this isn't a great time to bring this up," Skip yelled up at Max from the rear, "but how are the brakes on this thing?"

"I don't know," Max yelled back as they began to roll down the other side. "I've never tried—"

The rest of his sentence was lost in the wind as Piper and Karen screamed and the vehicle coasted to the bottom of the hill.

Finally the gates to the club, decorated with lanterns and strings of lights, glowed in the dark ahead of them. Just before they entered the drive, Max stopped the bike and turned to face them on his seat.

"There is one thing I forgot to mention," he began.

"I knew there'd be a catch!" Skip cracked.

"It's not a big one, Skipper," Max retorted with a grin. "It's just that we have to leave by midnight."

"Or what?" Karen cut in, giggling. "We turn into pumpkins?"

"Or else we get in trouble with the club," Max explained. "So we'll all meet outside at a quarter to twelve!"

"Just before the unmasking," Piper pointed out.

"Right!" Max said. "That way, they'll never know we were there."

"Since no one has brought it up," Skip called from the back, "I will. How do you plan to get us into this little shindig?"

Piper's heart leaped into her throat. "That's

right. They'll take one look at us and call the sheriff."

"Trust me! Just do as I do, when I do it!" That was all Max would say. He turned and led them down the long drive toward the entrance to the ballroom, which was off the terrace. Strings of miniature lights lit the way.

Two men in red coats and gloves stood on either side of the sidewalk, checking invitations from the line of costumed party-goers. Piper's heart stopped. The guards were two of the caddies from the golf course, Sean and Richard. They ate at the Deckhouse every day and would surely recognize her and Karen!

Max suddenly began pedaling faster, and the others automatically followed suit. The quadricycle gathered momentum and was soon rattling along at a terrific speed. Piper could see Sean and Richard look up in startled surprise as the strange contraption bore down on them.

Then Max tapped the long cane he had pulled from a bag attached to the handlebars. It burst into a long tricolored flag that rippled out over their heads like a streamer. Written on it in bold letters were the words "Clown Town." Max let loose a loud blast of his horn, Skip immediately squeezed his, Piper and Karen loudly rang their bells. As they swept by the startled gate-keepers, Max waved an official-looking piece of paper at them and shouted, "It's all right, we're the entertainment!"

Piper held her breath and waited for the inevitable "Stop!" from the guards. Instead, she heard applause! Looking quickly over her shoulder, Piper observed the guests waiting in line clapping enthusiastically and Sean and Richard grinning from ear to ear.

She breathed a huge sigh of relief. "Whatever that was," Piper said over Max's shoulder, "it worked. What's your secret?"

Max leaned back and whispered, "Blind luck!"

He steered the quadricycle onto the grass around the side of the main building, well out of sight of the redcoats. After Max and Skip stashed the 'cycle behind a large, manicured hedge, the quartet tiptoed back to the edge of the brightly lit terrace. Piper clapped her hands in delight.

A steady stream of masked revelers passed across the terrace and through the floral arch, all of them clad in gorgeous costumes. Inside, pairs of dancers flitted in and out of sight by the tall French windows.

"Well, Karen, we did it," Piper said slowly. "We're here!"

Max leaned forward and offered his arm to Piper. "Shall we?"

Piper nodded quickly and looped her arm

through his. She was too nervous and excited to say a word.

At the floral arch, twelve violinists, dressed in tuxedos, greeted them with an impromptu serenade. Inside, the white pillars in the ballroom were strung with garlands and floral bouquets, and two huge crystal chandeliers glittered above the swirling dancers on the parquet-tiled floor.

"It's everything I hoped it would be," Piper gasped. "And more!" Couples circled among the tables at one end of the room, playfully trying to discover who was behind each mask.

"Tyler, is that you?" A short guy, masked himself, with a black cape and hood, peered up at Max curiously. Immediately Piper recognized him as Royce Dowling, David Barkley's habitual tennis partner at the club.

"Wouldn't you like to know?" Max retorted.

"Come on, Tyler, quit kidding around," Royce persisted. Suddenly he caught sight of Piper by Max's side. Even through his mask, Piper could see his eyes widen with surprise. "Oh, I'm sorry, I must be mistaken!"

After Royce had disappeared back into the crush of people, Piper tugged on Max's sleeve. "What made him say that?" she whispered.

Max shrugged. "I don't know. He probably figured there was no way Tyler whoever-he-is could have gotten such a beautiful girl as his date."

Piper felt herself blush underneath her mask. "Come on," she said. "Let's go look at everyone!"

Max took her arm again, and they threaded their way among the tables. To Piper's surprise they drew a lot of attention. When she finally caught a glimpse of the two of them in the mirror, she realized why. They did make a perfect pair, like two china dolls on an antique clock. Even the colors in their clothes blended harmoniously. Max looked dashing and handsome in his harlequin costume. And with her hair pulled up in curls and her bodice making her waist look so tiny, Piper actually felt beautiful.

A man, also dressed in a red coat, entered the room and rang a tiny silver bell.

"Ladies and gentlemen," he announced, "the buffet is ready for your pleasure!"

A row of double doors swung open, and the revelers eagerly followed the man into the banquet room. Rows of tables ringed the walls, laden with elegantly prepared entrées and hors d'oeuvres.

"Max, look!" Piper exclaimed.

Between the tables, two silver punch bowls had been raised on platforms, ringed with crystal goblets. Each bowl was actually a fountain, with tiny streams of rose-colored punch cascading into the basin below. But it was the fabulous ice sculptures in the center of each bowl that excited Piper's attention.

"Amazing!" Max murmured in awe. "They're us!"

The statuettes were of Harlequin and his Columbine. Harlequin held a mandolin in his arms and was posed serenading his lady. Columbine had turned away discreetly, watching him over her shoulder with a coy smile. Max and Piper were dressed in the exact same style as the glistening figurines.

"Excuse me, miss," a familiar voice drawled from beside her. Piper jumped, a little startled, and moved quickly out of the way of the white-coated man in a chef's hat carrying a fresh supply of sliced beef.

"Sorry, Chester," Piper said as he slipped by.

At the sound of his name, Chester looked around at the milling crowd. It was clear he had not recognized her.

"It's me, Piper," she murmured under her breath. Then Piper dipped down into a grand curtsy, her skirt billowing out around her. Max bowed deeply from the waist.

Some of the other couples, still keeping their eyes on Piper and Max, thought Chester must be the famous chef, Pierre St. Juste, and politely applauded him.

The little man turned beet-red, absolutely flabbergasted. Impulsively he tucked one foot behind him and, grinning dizzily, made a clumsy curtsy instead of a bow. Then he winked at Piper and marched proudly out of the room.

"Gosh," Piper whispered to Max as he led her toward the buffet, "I'm too nervous to eat."

"We can get a bite later," Max agreed. "I think this was just the formal presentation of the banquet. Sort of the grand opening."

Just then the orchestra began a spirited number, and Max and Piper were swept along with the surge of people toward the dance floor.

"I have another idea," Max said when it became obvious they were not going to be able to escape the crush. "Let's dance!"

"I hope I remember everything I learned in Mrs. Clement's dancing school," Piper whispered.

Max pointed off to their left and grinned. Skip and Karen were already on the floor. Piper noticed with a smile that Skip did not seem to mind dancing with Karen at all.

"I believe this is a waltz," Max announced, taking Piper by one hand and wrapping the other around her waist. "All we have to do is count to three."

"Right!" They paused for a second, bobbing their heads in time and chanting, "One, two, three—one, two, three!"

Finally Max said, "Go!"

He swept Piper onto the dance floor, spinning in and out of the other dancers. The first time around, Piper kept mumbling, "One, two, three!"

under her breath. Then she realized Max knew what he was doing, and she let herself relax into his arms. One dance followed another, and another, and the endless twirling made Piper feel a little giddy. Or was it just happiness that made her feel that way? She couldn't tell.

Finally the orchestra paused for a break, and Skip and Karen appeared beside them, slightly out of breath.

"You guys must have practiced, to dance like that!" Karen said. Skip's arm was resting lightly on her shoulder, and Piper had never seen her look so happy.

"No, it's just chemistry," Max explained. He was still holding Piper's hand. "Dancing's not so bad, once you've found the right partner."

"Well, you've got everyone talking," Karen whispered, leaning in closer to Piper. "They're all trying to guess who you are!"

Piper felt exhilarated. There was a delicious freedom in being the mysterious stranger, the object of everyone's curiosity.

I could be anyone to these people tonight, she thought suddenly. *A debutante, an heiress— even a princess!*

A tall young man elegantly dressed as a cavalier appeared at her side and said, "May I have the pleasure of the next dance?"

Piper glanced over at Max, who waved his hand agreeably. "Go ahead. I'll get us some punch." He fanned his face with his hand. "A little of this dancing stuff goes a long way with me!"

Her confidence building with each moment, Piper answered the invitation with a dazzling smile and followed her new partner toward the dancers.

As they moved across the dance floor Piper sensed that there was something very familiar about this tall stranger. The confident way he walked, the bold angle of his jaw beneath the white mask—Piper knew she had met him before. She racked her brain trying to place him in her memory.

Then he turned to her and smiled—a stunning, perfect smile that left no mistaking his identity. Piper wanted to pinch herself to make sure it was not a dream. But this dream had come true. Piper suddenly realized she now had everything she ever wanted. She really was at the Harlequin Ball—and now she was about to dance with David Barkley.

Chapter Twelve

"Well?" Karen demanded eagerly, after David Barkley had returned Piper to the edge of the dance floor, politely thanked her, then disappeared into the crowd.

"Well, what?" Piper replied, looking out over the crowd for Max.

"Well, what's it feel like?"

"What are you talking about?" Piper asked, a perplexed look on her face.

"Don't play dumb with me!" Karen pulled Piper by the arm over to the edge of the room. "I'm talking about David Barkley, the Vision in White, the Man from Glad, Sir Lancelot, Mr. Wonderful, Mr.—"

"Mr. Dull," Piper finished for her.

"You're kidding!" Karen leaned against the wall in shock.

"You know," Piper continued with a smile, "he's very nice, very handsome, and very bland."

"I just can't believe it," Karen said.

"Well, it's true."

"Do you realize," Karen blurted out, "we have wasted ages drooling over a drip!"

Piper burst out laughing, and soon the two of them were giggling helplessly at how silly they had been.

"I don't think you've been giving David your undivided attention," Piper teased gently, pointing out into the crowd. Skip was working his way over to them, two glasses of punch in his hands.

Karen followed her friend's gaze, and giggled. "Well, you know what they say. 'A bird in the hand . . .' " She nudged Piper and said, "Look at how cute he is in that costume!"

Piper grinned as Karen drifted off to meet Skip. She spotted an empty chair at a nearby table and decided to rest her feet. But just as Piper was about to sit down, she felt a tap on her shoulder. Turning around, she saw a lion tamer gesturing toward the dance floor.

By the time Max was her partner again, Piper had danced with a Roman poet, a hooded monk, a turbaned rajah, and Zorro. The cavalier, also known as David Barkley, had danced with her again as well.

"Having a good time?" Max asked, deftly maneuvering them around a couple who were doing a flamboyant tango.

"The absolute best!" Piper trilled. "Oh, Max, this is the most incredible night of my life. I want it to go on forever!"

"I'm glad you're happy." Max looked out over the crowd toward the banquet room, then asked, "Hungry yet? The herd over at the trough seems to have thinned out a bit."

Piper shook her head. "You go ahead. I'll watch the dancing."

Before Max was out of sight, another boy asked her to dance. After a while Piper stopped looking for Max in the crowd and simply went from one partner to the next. There seemed to be no end to dancing. The glitter and glamour of the ball had her completely dazzled, and she happily surrendered to its spell.

Finally there was a lull and Piper excused herself from the next dance, insisting she had to catch her breath.

"Piper," a voice whispered by her side. It was Max. "Piper, it's a quarter to twelve. Time to go."

"Oh, no!" she protested. "We can't go home! Not yet!"

"Listen, the unmasking is at midnight," Max explained patiently. "We've got to be gone by then."

"Oh, Max, that's ridiculous!" Piper said. "Everyone's been so nice—they wouldn't really throw us out!"

"I don't think I really want to test your theory," Max replied, pulling her gently toward the exit. Piper dug in her heels and stopped.

"Max, the party is going to go on for hours more," she pleaded. "And I don't want to miss a minute of it!"

"Look, Piper, it's not up to you," Max insisted. "I told you the rules before we came in—"

"Oh, I get it!" Piper flared angrily. "You just want to leave because you're bored. You never liked this kind of party, anyway. You said so yourself!"

"That's not it at all," Max retorted, stepping back from her. "How can you say that?"

Piper was not listening. All she knew was that this was the greatest night of her life, and she intended to make the most of it.

"You guys can do what you like," she declared. "I'm staying. Nothing's going to happen."

Piper started to turn away, but Max caught her by the arm. "Please, Piper, listen to me! We'll wait for you by the hedge until midnight, okay?"

A masked figure tapped Max on the shoulder. It was David Barkley again.

"Mind if I cut in?" David asked formally.

"No, not at all," Max replied. He was looking meaningfully at Piper and said, "I was just leaving."

David led Piper by the hand toward the dance

floor. Piper couldn't help looking back over her shoulder at Max. He hadn't moved a muscle.

He's just kidding, she thought suddenly. *It's all a joke.*

As she and David swept around the floor Piper caught glimpses of Max in the crowd. He stared at her for a long time, his colorful costume easily visible among the other guests'. Just before she and David danced around one of the white pillars at the end of the hall, he raised one hand, as if waving good-bye. When they emerged from the other side, Max was gone.

He couldn't have meant it! Piper thought. *The night has barely begun!*

"Ouch!" Piper cried out at a sharp pain on her instep.

"I'm really sorry," David apologized, pausing to see if she was all right.

"No, no, it was my fault," Piper heard herself saying. *I'll have a bruise tomorrow*, she thought and mused on how much she could tell about a guy from the way he danced. David danced exactly the way he looked—starched and ironed. Nothing out of place, totally predictable. On the other hand, Max seemed instinctively to know how to move with her, impulsively, without planning too much. And that made it fun.

"Then we'll all get a chance to see who you are!" David's voice intruded loudly into her thoughts.

"I'm sorry," Piper said. "What did you say?"

"The unmasking," he explained. "The guys have all taken bets on your real identity."

Piper froze in the middle of the floor as David added with a chuckle, "The winner gets to dance with you for the rest of the evening!"

"Don't I have any say in this?" Piper asked, stepping back from him.

"Well, sure—" he stammered, confused by her response.

Suddenly Piper no longer felt flattered by all the attention. The ball was still in full swing, but the thrill was gone. Max was gone. And she wanted to go, too.

A fanfare went up from the orchestra and the Master of Revels stepped onto the platform. He was an older man, dressed up as Benjamin Franklin. As soon as he began to speak, Piper recognized him as Mr. Sinclair, the president of the club.

"Ladies and gentlemen, it is now three minutes to twelve," he announced. "Prepare yourselves for the unmasking!"

A cheer went up, and Piper's heart pounded in her chest. She tried to back inconspicuously toward the ladies' lounge. "There she is!" a boy's voice sounded from beside her.

Piper instantly bolted the other way toward the front entrance. She could hear the crowd counting "Five-four-three-two" when she reached the floral arch. Just as she was about to step through it, a pudgy hand grabbed her arm.

"Excuse me, miss," she heard a polite voice say. "Allow me to escort you to your car."

Piper looked up and almost fainted. Standing beside her was Mr. Wallace. *This is it*, she thought. *This is where I lose my job.*

At the front door, the red-liveried attendant raised a gloved hand to his hat. Over his shoulder, Piper spotted a white Mercedes pulling up in front of the club.

Without hesitating, Piper turned to Mr. Wallace and said, "Here's my car now. Thank you so much. It's been a lovely ball."

With that, she threw open the back door of the Mercedes, slid across the leather seat, and waved politely. Mr. Wallace jauntily saluted, then adjusted his tie, and went back inside the Club.

As soon as he was out of sight, Piper threw open the door on the other side of the car and stepped outside.

"Thanks for the lift," Piper whispered to the bewildered driver. Then she gathered up her skirts and disappeared into the darkness.

Chapter Thirteen

Piper edged down the drive as stealthily as she could, ducking behind the thick hedge to avoid the headlights of passing cars. She slipped through the gate onto the main road and turned around to take one last look at the Harlequin Ball.

The music, now faint and distant, rang softly in the cool night air. The strings of lights hanging across the terrace beside the ballroom twinkled like delicate stars. Occasionally, a burst of merry laughter lifted up into the night sky and echoed across the grounds.

Piper bit back a tear, realizing that, for her, the ball was truly over. She was feeling in her pocket for a handkerchief when a gray shadow fell across her path. She looked up, startled.

There, silhouetted starkly against the moonlit sky, was Max. His Harlequin costume glittered richly in the silvery light.

"May I?" He pulled a handkerchief from the sleeve of his doublet and held it out to Piper. The movement made a lock of his unruly hair slip down over one eye. Piper thought he looked wonderful.

"Thank you," Piper whispered, gratefully taking the handkerchief and dabbing at her eyes. A small silence followed. Finally Piper asked, a little timidly, "Where are Skip and Karen?"

"They went on ahead with the quadricycle." He looked down at the ground. "I think they wanted to be alone."

"Max," Piper asked in a quiet voice, "why did you stay?"

"You didn't think I'd let you walk home by yourself, did you?"

"I wouldn't blame you," Piper said, twisting the handkerchief in her hand. "Especially after the way I behaved."

"Did you have a good time?" Max cocked his head to one side.

"Oh, Max, it was wonderful!" Piper's eyes glistened as she said, "Everything was just as I'd imagined. It would have been perfect, if—" She paused, remembering her harsh words to him.

"If what?" he prodded gently.

"If I hadn't been so selfish." Piper ruefully

shook her head. "I don't know what came over me. I'm sorry."

"Well, it's over now," Max said gently. He stepped into the road and offered her his arm. "Miss Piper Elliot, may I escort you home?"

Piper curtsied and replied formally, "Yes, you may, Mister Max—" A bewildered look crossed her face, and she asked, "Max who?"

"What?" Now Max looked perplexed.

Piper giggled and explained. "Max, this may sound silly, but I don't know your last name."

"Oh"—he chuckled—"it's Cavanaugh."

"Max Cavanaugh?" Piper tried the name out loud.

"Well, actually"—Max took a deep breath—"it's Milton Artemus Cavanaugh the Third."

"You're kidding!" Piper laughed, covering her mouth and trying to stop herself.

"See?" He pointed at her in mock indignation and backed away down the road. "That's why I'd rather be called Max!"

Piper raced to catch up with him. "I'm sorry, Max." She giggled. "It's just so—unusual."

They continued down the road when Piper suddenly stopped. "You know, there's something familiar about your name." She cocked her head to look at him. "I think I've heard it somewhere before."

"Not from me, you haven't!"

"Wait a minute." Piper snapped her fingers.

"On the membership list!" She put her hands on her hips and said accusingly, "Max, you're a member of the club!"

"Correction! My *family* joined the club, but I don't go there."

"I don't understand," Piper's mind was reeling. "Why didn't you tell me who you were?"

"You never asked."

"But you said you dug clams for a living."

"No." Max shook his head. "I met Skip out clamming, and *you* decided that's what I did for a living. So I went along with it." He shrugged sheepishly. "I thought it would be a good way to get to know you."

"What?" Piper asked. "By lying to me?"

"No." Max took her hand in his and said, "I wanted you to get to know me and, hopefully, like me for myself—not my family's name."

"Max"—Piper looked up at him thoughtfully—"you're rich, aren't you?"

"Yes," he said simply. "Does that make a difference?"

"Well, of course it does!" she exclaimed. A mischievous glint shone in her eyes. "You owe me a lobster dinner, buddy! Now I won't feel guilty about asking you to pay up."

Max burst out laughing. Impulsively he lifted her off the ground and spun her around in his arms. "Piper Elliot," Max declared softly, as he set her back on her feet, "you are something else!"

"And don't you forget it. Milton Artemus Cavanaugh the Third!" Max winced as she recited his full name, and Piper giggled.

They strolled hand in hand down the ribbon of road, the sea breeze rushing through Piper's hair. The moonlit shapes of the beautiful summer homes of North Harbor slipped by them as they walked.

"Max," Piper said, stopping in front of a massive wrought-iron gateway. "I just have one question."

"Fire away."

"Why did we go through that big charade tonight at the gate, when you could have gotten us an invitation to the ball?"

"Because that would be breaking the rule," Max replied.

"What rule?"

"Cavanaugh's Rule. Never buy your way into anything."

He grinned at her confusion. "My grandfather, Milton Artemus Cavanaugh the Second— also known as Max—came up with it. Gramps prizes ingenuity over everything. He built the quadricycle."

"I'd like to meet your grandfather," Piper said with a laugh.

"You can," he replied. He turned to Piper and

grasped her gently by the shoulders. "I just know Gramps will love you," he said, his voice suddenly low and husky. "Because I do."

"Oh, Max!" Piper murmured. She reached up and smoothed a stray lock of his hair back from his forehead. "I've been wanting to do that all evening," she confessed shyly.

Max pressed her hand to his cheek and then kissed it tenderly. He bent forward and pulled her toward him.

"I've been wanting to do this since we met," Max said, his eyes shining with a special glow.

His lips met hers in a soft, lingering kiss. They stood close together, not wanting to break away. Piper closed her eyes and rested her head against his shoulder.

"I could stay here forever," she whispered. "I'm so happy."

"That's fine with me." Max brushed her lips again. "Because we're home."

Piper opened her eyes dreamily and looked around her. With a start, she recognized the gates beside them.

"It's not possible!" Piper whispered. There, glowing through the trees, stood the familiar gray and white mansion, its windows ablaze with light.

"You live here?"

Max nodded and slipped his arm around her waist.

Piper shook her head in amazement.

"Anything wrong?" Max asked.

Piper leaned her head against his shoulder and murmured softly, "Nothing's wrong. It's just that—" She looked up into his brown eyes again and smiled.

"You know, Max, sometimes dreams really do come true."

He leaned down and kissed her again. Then, together, they followed the carpet of moonlight up to Sea Cliff.